Philip Threadneedle wrc
in the Canteen, when he
It was six pages long. You'll be delighted to
hear that *The Astronaut's Apprentice* is even
longer, and every bit as exciting.

You can reach the author by sending an e-mail
to philipthreadneedle@falconberger.co.uk.

THE ASTRONAUT'S APPRENTICE

BY PHILIP THREADNEEDLE

Falcon Berger

A Falcon Berger book
www.falconberger.co.uk
published by arrangement with the author

ISBN: 1453843809
EAN-13: 9781453843802

This book is a work of fiction. People, places, events, and situations are the product of the author's imagination. Any resemblance to actual persons, living or dead, or historical events, is purely coincidental.

Set in fonts created by Ray Larabie
www.larabiefonts.com

10 9 8 7 6 5 4 3 2 1

This book is dedicated to Mum and Dad,

with love

Chapters

A Night At Home With

Grandma

ONE NIGHT—ONE dark, howling night—Grandma put down her knitting, cleared her throat, and began to tell a story.

"You know everyone raves about *the miracle of childbirth*," she began bitterly. "Well *I* think it's the most overrated thing in the world. I didn't enjoy giving birth to your father, and from the look on his face, I'd say *he* didn't like it much either. Here! Are you listening, Bradley?"

He looked up at her. Before he could reply, the wind seized and shook the loose window, making raindrops dance on the dark glass.

"Listening?" he wondered bleakly. "Listening to what?"

She rolled her eyes.

"I was telling a story!" she complained. "Now listen! People always rave about *the miracle of childbirth*," she began again—but Bradley groaned, and held up a hand to stop her.

"I don't want to hear one of your *horrible stories*," he said grumpily. "I'm going to bed. You can tell me tomorrow."

He made to rise, but she reached out and grabbed him.

"Sit down!" she growled.

Lightning went off at the window, seeming to take a flash photograph of the room. Bradley lowered himself unhappily onto the carpet.

"Now listen," she snapped. "A baby, generally speaking—your average newborn baby—is *not* pleased to be here. Stands to reason. I mean, where would *you* rather be?" She beamed and patted her tummy. "Nice and cosy in there, I'm sure! Or used to be. Prob'ly full of cobwebs now. Hang on."

She resumed her knitting. *CLICKETTY-CLACK!* went the needles. They made Bradley shudder.

When she knitted, she reminded him of a praying mantis, rubbing its horrible long hands over some smaller insect. The strange thing was, she never seemed to actually *make* anything. Just a shapeless woollen tube that got longer and longer, coming to bits around her bony ankles.

"Grandma?" he ventured.

She didn't reply. He began to wonder if he was free to go, and inched quietly towards the door on his bottom.

"When your father was born," she suddenly resumed—squinting through the tangled mess of wool—"he did *not* look impressed. Can't blame him either. It's bad enough getting out of bed in the morning. Imagine being born! Then they took him away to be examined, and that was the last I saw of him for a month."

Lightning popped a second time. Bradley frowned as the thunder came rumbling after it.

"An entire month? *That's* not normal," he pointed out.

Grandma nodded.

"Right. But neither was your father. He came in at nine pounds. A bouncing baby boy with a full head of hair."

Bradley picked at the carpet.

"Sounds pretty normal to me," he muttered.

"Well on the surface, yes. But the weird thing is, I'd only been pregnant for a fortnight. And that was just the start of it! A month later, he was already walking and talking. By about age eight, I'd say he looked exactly like he does now, except his hair was brown instead of grey. What do you make of that?"

Bradley stared at her, then shook his head.

"No way," he said firmly. "You're pulling my leg. That's *too* weird."

She leaned back in her chair looking very pleased with herself.

"Cross my heart!" she promised him.

She dragged a single sharp nail across her chest, and a strange light twinkled in her eyes.

"After all," she reminded him, in a dark, dark voice—"we're a pretty weird family. Don't you think?"

* * *

Were they weird, wondered Bradley?

His schoolmates lived in a nearby town. *He*
didn't. He lived in a windswept farm with a
view of the mountains.

It was a high, giddy sort of place. A place
where the air was fresh but never warm, and
you could see for miles in all directions.

It was a desolate place. Trestle tables rotted
in the long grass. Pennants flapped from the
bony trees. A rusty tombola had filled with
rain. There was even a hoopla stall, warped by
years of sun and rain but still standing. Some
nights, when the far-off peaks began to darken,
Bradley liked to play hoopla. He would toss
hoop after hoop at the old glass jars, hearing
them *DINK!* and deflect.

There were other things in the long grass
too—other, much stranger things. There were
things with buttons and dials, for instance, and
long antennae that pointed at the sky. Whatever
they were, they were covered in rust and half-
buried in moss—but some nights, if Bradley

went to the window, he could see their little red lights blinking in the darkness.

Once, he caught Grandma inspecting them in the rain with her trousers tucked into her socks. She jumped when she saw him and refused to explain what she was doing. *That* was pretty weird.

Another time, Bradley had been taken to see a doctor, but no one would tell him why. Instead of going to the surgery in town, they drove him to a large country house and marched him to a tiny bright room at the back of it. A crabby old doctor had prodded him around for half an hour, occasionally breaking the silence to ask, "Well? Got anything *weird* you want to show me, laddy? Like—I don't know—any *tentacles* you can shoot out the top of your head, anything like that?"

At the end of the interview, the doctor had simply collapsed back into his chair, saying, "Well! He's not weird at all! Take him away, the little time-waster!"—which made Bradley conclude that he probably *was* weird, whatever the doctor said.

Sometimes, Bradley would stand in the school toilets, peering at his scalp in the mirror. He told people that he was looking for nits. He was actually looking for tentacles. Other times, he would squeeze all the muscles in his head until his skull vibrated, trying to make long squiddy tentacles *squomp* out of it. All he ever got was a headache.

Meanwhile, back in the present, Grandma had stopped her knitting. She put the needles to one side and flexed her fingers very carefully, making a horrible noise like popcorn popping.

"*Well?*" she said tartly

Bradley stared unhappily at his feet. There was no point denying it. They *were* weird—just like Grandma said.

But why?

Deep down, he'd always wondered.

"You see," explained Grandma eventually, blinking eyes the colour of nacho cheese at him—"you've never noticed how *weird* this family is because your father and I are good at keeping secrets. But we *are* weird. Take yourself," she suggested, jabbing a knitting needle towards him. "Why—you're even weirder than your father!"

"What? *Me* weirder? Shut up!" he replied hotly. "I'm completely normal. The doctor said so."

"Exactly," agreed Grandma. "Completely normal. And if you knew what was in your *genes,* Bradley, you'd understand just how weird that makes you! There are things in that *double-helix* of yours that would *make your blood curdle*—if only you knew!"

Bradley's mouth went suddenly dry, so he licked his lips.

"Like what?" he asked.

But she had run out of steam. She just frowned and looked at her knitting.

"Where was I?" she wondered at last.

Bradley pinched the bridge of his nose and counted to ten.

"Genes," he told her firmly. "You were telling

me about my *genes.*"

Her eyes widened.

"*Genes?*" she repeated—and suddenly, she became agitated. "Forget about those!" she snapped. "Genes, indeed! Take my advice, Bradley—don't ever go tracing your family tree. You won't like what you find. No, sir!"

Then she seized her knitting, and went about it so wildly that you could hardly call it knitting any more. The needles flashed like long knives, and before long, the air was a blizzard of floating fibres.

Bradley groaned and batted them away from his face.

"Great," he said sarcastically, getting up from the floor. "Well I guess I'll be going to bed now. Night night, Grandma."

She froze.

"What? Wait!" she croaked. "I've not finished with you yet!"

She threw the needles away and leaned forward, licking her dry lips.

"Do you want to know a secret?" she offered

suddenly. "A big, juicy secret? Because if you promise not to tell," she added with relish, "I happen to know a secret that will *turn your hair white.*"

He paused, turned slowly to face her, and nodded.

"Promise," he assured her.

She didn't look convinced.

"Cross your heart and hope to die?"

He raised a hand and crossed it very solemnly.

"Excellent!" she rasped. "Now listen. I'm going to take you upstairs to where your *father* keeps something *very odd.* It'll change how you look at everything! But," she decided, looking him up and down, "I think you're ready."

She rocked a few times, trying to get out of the chair.

"Help me up!" she barked, holding out her bony arms.

He did exactly that. He walked her to the door—and then, threading his arm through the bony crook of her elbow, helped her up the dark stairs.

THE THING IN THE ATTIC

WHEN THEY GOT to the top of the stairs, Grandma pointed at a hatch in the ceiling.

"We're going up there," she told him. "Into the loft. I want to show you something that your Dad keeps secret!"

As she spoke, her eyes fell on the extending ladder which lay along the wall. She grunted and gave it a kick.

"You need to get this ladder and put it under the hatch," she added. "Chop chop!"

Bradley looked annoyed but wrestled with it anyway.

"This is *not* a good idea," he muttered, getting it upright. "Dad always says that the attic isn't safe. You could put your foot through the ceiling and all sorts."

But Grandma shook her head.

"Nonsense," she said firmly. "There's something up there that your Dad doesn't want you to see—that's all. Now open the hatch!"

Bradley mounted the ladder. *SQUAWK, SQUAWK, SQUAWK!* went the rungs. When he reached the top, he clutched the ladder with one hand, reached above his head with the other, and gave the trapdoor a good hard shove. It reared like a horse and toppled back on its hinges.

THUMP! it went at last.

There. The hatch was open.

A cold draught descended from the dark. One by one, the hairs began to rise on Bradley's neck.

"So what now?" he wondered—trying to keep the tremor from his voice.

Grandma was picking her nose. She inspected her finger, then flicked something gory over the side of the landing.

"There should be a pull-cord to turn the light on," she replied—wiping her hands on her thighs. "Is it there?"

20

Bradley gritted his teeth and reached up into the dark opening. As he did, something horrible occurred to him. What if cold fingers were to reach down and *grab* his wrist? He performed a half-hearted sweep of the interior, then pulled his hand out as fast as he could.

"Nope," he said nervously—rubbing his arm. "So what now? Back downstairs?"

Grandma rolled her eyes.

"You've got a head, haven't you? Well use it! Fetch a torch!" she croaked.

Bradley groaned, then climbed down the ladder and popped his head into the master bedroom. When he felt for the light switch, nothing happened.

His heart sank. The bulb had blown.

Even with the door open, the room was very dark. The wardrobe in the corner seemed to radiate menace.

But that was where Dad kept his torch.

"Hurry up!" called Grandma behind him.

"All right, all right!" he growled. "Give me a second."

He gritted his teeth and stepped into the room. Nothing happened. Then he clambered onto the enormous bed, waded across it on his knees, climbed down beside the tall wooden wardrobe, and threw the double doors wide open.

Inside, Dad's dark suits were like bodies hanging in a freezer. The shoes were like enormous black beetles snoozing below. Behind the shoes, at the back of the wardrobe, were some tools in a dirty metal box. Bradley pulled it out and lifted the lid, revealing (among other things) a small torch.

"Got it!" he called.

He returned to the landing with the prize in his hands. Grandma snatched it from him, hitched up her skirt, and began to climb the ladder.

"Wait till I get to the top," she barked. "This piece of junk won't hold two of us!"

Bradley held his breath, terrified that she would lose her grip and fall. He knew that she was very old, and she would often say that her bones were as brittle as bread sticks. If she fell, she would probably break in a thousand places—and how would he explain that to Dad?

Luckily, after what seemed like hours, she managed to haul her old body to the top of the ladder and safely through the hatch.

"Follow me!" she called at last.

Bradley shivered as he mounted the ladder and did exactly that.

A few seconds later, he popped his head into the loft. It was very musty up there and ice cold, and something mechanical huffed and puffed in the darkness.

"Grandma?" he called nervously.

But Grandma was lost in the maze of old junk. She swung the torch this way and that, searching for something in the gloom. All Bradley could see of her was an occasional flash of torch light.

"Wait there!" she called. Her voice sounded very muffled. "I'll let you know when I've found it."

Bradley scanned the floor and spotted a pile of old comics. He smiled. It wasn't so bad in the loft after all! He began to inspect the bags and old boxes, looking for more treasure. There were star charts and telescopes and Thermos flasks. He moved some mouldy old cushions and found a free standing model of the Solar System. The planets were made out of tin, and the sun was a dusty light bulb in the centre of the table.

He found a switch and turned it on. The sun lit up each of the ten planets, turning their moons into tiny crescents.

Hang on, he suddenly thought. *Ten* planets?

He counted them quickly. Yes, ten. Pluto was on there, even though it had since been relegated from the list. It was like a garden pea beside the oranges and apples of the gas giants. But there was another one beyond that—dark and mysterious, and at least as large as the Earth. The light from the dim bulb barely reached it.

Before Bradley could investigate further, he

was interrupted by Grandma.

"Bradley!" she called. "Where are you? I've found it!"

"I'm here," he replied—homing in on the sound of her voice. He made his way through a corridor of boxes, climbed a pile of carpets, and found her on the other side of an old shower curtain. She shone the torch at his face, temporarily blinding him.

"Remember," she warned—"not a word to anyone!"

Then she let the beam settle on something—he wasn't sure what—but as his vision returned, he could see that it glittered darkly, and feel the cold air coming off it.

"Come closer," she told him.

She backed off a little to let the beam spread, revealing more and more of the strange exhibit for Bradley to see. As she did, her breath shone like smoke in the cold air, becoming an aerosol of silver droplets.

Bradley stood and stared.

It was a glittering steel cabinet with cranks

and chrome gears, and a giant accordion breathing beside it. The cabinet itself had a glass front, but Bradley couldn't see into it, because it was covered in frost and steaming coldly. It was like a weird sarcophagus, or maybe an escape pod. It stood before him, humming darkly with its own power.

"Come here!" snapped Grandma. Her teeth were beginning to chatter. "I want you to see this."

The air got colder and colder as he walked towards it, until it actually hurt his teeth to inhale.

"But what is it?" he wondered.

"See for yourself!" she replied. She scrubbed a window in the frost and stepped aside.

Bradley went to peer through the cold glass.

Then he gasped and turned quite pale.

Finally, he turned to Grandma.

"You're in *big trouble* now," he said quietly.

Because, entombed in the glittering coffin, was *the body of a woman.*

She was as crisp and as white as a winter

lawn, with blue lips and brittle hair. Tears had frozen beneath her eyes like tiny white pearls.

"I think you'd better tell me *exactly what's going on* here," added Bradley, tapping the glass, "and why you've got a dead woman in this— well—whatever it is."

Grandma rolled her eyes.

"It's a *Cryo-Genie*. Keeps dead people fresh indefinitely. And if you *must* know," she added, "the dead woman inside it *happens* to be your mother."

Bradley was speechless.

"My *mother?*" he managed at last.

Already, the little view hole was steaming over. He raised a hand to wipe it, and was surprised to find that the glass vibrated to the touch— humming with strange power.

Grandma nodded.

"Your mother. She's been hiding up here for a long, long time."

Bradley leaned forward. Suddenly, he realised that the woman was wearing a wedding veil. She had a snow-white dress to match, and her hands were folded on a bridal bouquet.

"But what's she doing up here?" he wondered.

Grandma blew her nose. Suddenly, her rubbery wrinkles shone with tears. Then she wiped them away and composed herself.

"You were just a baby," she began. "I remember it like it was yesterday. Your father went to the funeral home and came back with a leaflet. *Deals so good,*" she remembered brightly, *"that you'll dance on their graves."*

"Charming," muttered Bradley.

Grandma didn't hear him.

"We sat downstairs and tried to decide what to do with her. They did all sorts of fancy things, like burial at sea or putting your ashes in a rocket, but your father just wanted to have her buried. You know—interred."

Bradley looked at her in horror.

"He wanted to have her *buried in turd?*" he gasped.

"That's right," agreed Grandma. "But then he changed his mind. Decided it would be better if he kept her fresh with *cryogenics.* Reckoned that, if he waited for his own dad to come home, then—"

She broke off awkwardly and shook her head.

"But that's another story," she said firmly.

Bradley rubbed his arms and shivered. His eyes wandered to the pale face—the frosty veil—the thin blue lips.

"But why did nobody *tell* me?" he asked in a small voice. "Sometimes I feel—"

Before he could continue, Grandma became irate.

"Feel?" she snapped. "Feel? What makes you think I want to hear about your *feelings?* Who do you think I am—your personal therapist?"

He was taken aback.

"But I was just going to ask—"

She started to shoo him away.

"Go on!" she cried. "Leave me! Leave me to my memories!"

"Well *honestly,*" muttered Bradley—but he did as he was told. He paused briefly by the shower curtain and watched her sobbing quietly. She pressed her hands and face to the icy glass, not realising that he could still see her.

He didn't like to watch, so he climbed over the carpets and made his way back to the hatch. Before he ducked out of earshot, he realised that Grandma had stopped crying and was talking bitterly to herself.

"Oh, Grandma," she was saying—"you old fool! Well, your mother did warn you, but did you listen? Oh, no! You had to *run away,* didn't you? Had to *marry an alien,* didn't you? Oh—what a stupid, stupid girl you are!"

Bradley was so surprised that he let go of the ladder.

Some minutes later, groaning softly to himself, he picked himself up off the landing and limped to bed.

BRAIN-O-MATIC SUPER-TAP

THAT NIGHT, BRADLEY lay awake for a long, long time, staring at the ceiling in a sort of stunned stupor. His head was full of wild thoughts. All his life, there had been two gaps in his family tree—and deep down, without really knowing it, he had yearned for answers. Now he had them. Grandpa was an alien, and Mum was dead in the loft.

Not exactly cheery stuff, but still. Answers.

Finally—exhausted—he fell asleep.

KNOCKY-KNOCK-KNOCK! went the window quite suddenly.

He woke with a start and stared groggily around him.

"What?—oh—of course," he muttered, rubbing his eyes. "Must be Dad."

Dad was quite forgetful, and whenever he forgot his keys, he would take a bit of old broom handle from behind the bins and knock on Bradley's window.

KNOCKY-KNOCK-KNOCK! went the window again.

It was a familiar knock. The family knock, they called it.

Bradley climbed out of bed and went to the window, yawning and smacking his lips. The carpet felt cool beneath his bare toes, and according to the digital alarm clock, it was very nearly midnight.

When he got to the window, he reached for the dark curtain and yanked it aside. *And then he screamed. His jaw dropped with terror.*

He fell backwards with fright, and began to scrabble away from the window.

There was something looking in.

It wasn't human.

Hovering outside, bobbing around and peering through the glass, was a horrible humanoid *something*. It had flashing red eyes and an ugly dark grill instead of a mouth.

"Bradley!" it cried in a harsh robotic voice. "Open the window!"

Bradley was astonished.

"Open the—? Good grief! I most certainly will *not* open the window!" he replied indignantly.

"But Bradley!" rasped the horrible creature. "I've got something to tell you!"

Bradley continued to scrabble away across the carpet.

"You can tell me through the window," he suggested.

"But Bradley!"

"For goodness' sake! What?"

The monster pawed at the glass. It had horrible brass hands with big shiny knuckles.

"You won't be able to hear me," it pointed out, "unless you open the window."

Bradley was having none of it.

"I can hear you fine," he insisted.

"But look! Bradley!" cried the stranger.

There was a long, long pause.

"What?" snapped Bradley eventually.

The monster just peered through the window.

"Can't see a thing," it muttered at last.

It reached up with both hands, seeming to feel for something under its chin. Then it somehow *slid its whole face backwards,* revealing a grizzled chin and a warm smile, and a huge moustache that sprang out of nowhere.

"Much better!" cried the stranger, wringing sweat from his whiskers. The mask sat on his head like a hat. "Now. Where was I?"

Bradley stared at him.

"Where *were* you?" he said tartly. "Where *were* you? Don't you think it would be polite to introduce yourself, before you bombard me with all these questions?"

The old man bobbed around, looking pleased with himself.

"*Introduce* myself? What—as in, tell you who I am?"

He dropped from sight. Seconds later, he reappeared at the window.

"Well can't you guess?"

Bradley got off the floor and back into bed.

"If you don't tell me who you are," he said, pulling the duvet up to his chin, "then I'm just going to close my eyes and go to sleep. And you can bob around all you want, because I for one won't be paying attention."

The old man burst out laughing.

"Bob around?" he cried. *"Bob around?* I'm not *bobbing around,* dear boy. Ducks and apples bob around. What *I'm* doing is something quite special. Watch!"

He drew back from the window, proudly showing off the fact that he was sitting in a *little flying saucer.* As he got further away, he wrestled with a joystick, bashing the button with his free hand.

Suddenly, the saucer backfired and flashed all over like a fruit machine.

"Bradley!" cried the stranger, lurching around. He tried to lean forward, almost capsizing the little saucer. "Don't you get it? It's me! Grandpa!"

And he did a death-defying roll, hanging by his knees like a monkey.

Bradley rolled his eyes.

"Right!" he said, getting back out of bed. "Now *that* makes sense."

And he opened the window, shaking his head with amazement.

In no time at all, Grandpa had climbed inside and made himself comfy on the bed. It was after midnight, and Bradley felt very strange. Here he was, wide-awake in the middle of the night, talking to his long-lost alien Grandpa! The mask, apparently, was part of a strange space suit, which was mostly made of brass and black rubber. The horrible hands were just gauntlets, which came off to reveal normal fingers.

"Not a bad old place," began Grandpa, looking around. "One gee." He bounced lightly on the bed and looked satisfied. "That's just the right amount."

While he talked, Bradley studied his warm face and friendly wrinkles, trying to work out who he looked like. His eyes were like Dad's, except deeper, and warmer, and full of stars.

"Now where was I? Ah yes. The second I found out I was a father," he was saying, "I did a three point turn and flew straight back to Earth. But in space, nothing's ever simple. It took a long, long time for the news to reach me, and I was shipwrecked on the way back. By the time I got here, your father was all grown up. He had absolutely no interest in seeing space with me. He'd just met a girl, you see."

Bradley nodded eagerly.

"Right—a girl. I bet that was Mum."

Grandpa beamed at him.

"Of course! Your mother! How is she?"

Bradley looked at the floor.

"She's dead," he replied.

Then he remembered something.

"Oh, but listen!—I think Dad wanted you to *bring her back to life*. When you came back, I mean. He's got her frozen in the loft, all ready. That must be what Grandma meant!"

Grandpa looked alarmed at the idea, then

pulled a face and quickly changed the topic.

"Bring her back to life? Well, that's quite a challenge—all kinds of *variables* to consider, and whatnot—but we can talk about that another time, can't we? Eh? And anyway, back to the story—he was fairly civil with me, but to cut a long story short, he sent me packing."

Bradley tried to interrupt, but Grandpa carried on regardless.

"Well within his rights I suppose. I've hardly been a model dad, so I can't really blame him for showing me the door. But it gets lonely out there. And after I left, it was lonelier than ever. So years later, when I heard about a grandchild—and by that, I mean you—I came back as fast as I could."

He smiled at Bradley.

"You were very very young," he told him. "Much too young to be an astronaut. So I decided to go away, and come back when you'd grown up a bit. But I *did* intend to come back. You'd go crazy if you spent too much time alone—especially *out there*."

He paused, lost with his memories. Bradley forgot, momentarily, about the matter of his mother. He followed Grandpa's gaze across the room and through the window, to where brilliant stars lay scattered on the sky. Suddenly, a shiver zoomed up his body, electrifying his spine. What must it be like, he wondered, to be all alone in space?

"So what happened?" he pressed.

Grandpa was miles away.

"Mm? What happened? Oh—well—I *did* come back! And here I am! And I need an apprentice, dear boy. An apprentice," he explained, cracking his knuckles, "to learn the proud old trade of *being an astronaut.*"

Bradley was stunned. Grandpa's face was very close to his, and he could see little green veins in the corners of his eyes.

"Of course," added Grandpa, sounding suddenly serious—"if you find all this space stuff *traumatic,* I can make it so you never saw me. Hang on."

He groped inside his suit and pulled out a strange gadget. It was just like a bath tap, but had a moulded rubber handle and crazy flashing lights all over it.

"This is my *Brain-O-Matic Super-Tap*," he explained—holding it right under Bradley's nose. "Absolute *state of the art* in zapping your brain. All I have to do is twist the top, and *bang!*—you can wave goodbye to the last hour. So what do you say? Yes to a tour of the Solar System—or no, and you get a dose of this?"

Bradley wrinkled his nose at the strange object.

"A tour?" he wondered. "But where would we go?"

"Wherever we want," promised Grandpa. "The Canals of Mars, or the boutiques of the Asteroid Belt! Or maybe we'll go even further. Beyond the great Gas Giants, to the starlit shores of Grabelon!"

Bradley looked up at him.

"Grab a what?" he wondered stupidly.

"Grabelon!" replied Grandpa. He got up and

went to the window, pointing in a vague direction. "My home planet," he explained. "Number ten—just after Pluto."

As if by magic, as he pointed, a shooting star flared briefly in the sky, seeming to shoot from the tip of his finger. Bradley blinked, wondering if his eyes were playing tricks on him.

"But there's only *nine* planets," he protested. "In fact, there's only eight. Pluto got relegated."

Grandpa shook his head.

"There's more than that. A lot more. Some are very small. I know of one particular planet that is smaller than your head. I know of another," he added—in a dangerous whisper that made the hairs rise on the back of Bradley's neck—"that is *scarcely the size of a small garden pea*. Others, like Grabelon, are hidden."

Bradley wondered how it was possible to *hide* a planet. Then he remembered the model in the attic, with the tenth planet far from the sun. Still—it was far-fetched, to say the least.

"I don't think you could hide a whole planet," he muttered, half to himself. "And I'm *positive* there's only eight or nine."

Grandpa looked annoyed and rolled his eyes.

"Of course. Silly me! What was I thinking? I must have hallucinated an entire childhood for myself on a non-existent planet! I'm sure I'm actually from Leicester, or somewhere else perfectly normal."

Then his face softened.

"Look. Make your decision. I've got a shiny new spaceship in orbit right now. How about you and I take a little trip in it?"

He beamed beneath his moustache, making it fan like a deck of playing cards. Bradley looked at the Brain-O-Matic Super-Tap, wondering if it would hurt to have his memory wiped. Grandpa tossed it from hand to hand, testing its weight in a way that made it seem curiously threatening.

Suddenly, Bradley remembered what the old man was offering him. Why was he even hesitating?

"I'm sorry," he said, grinning weakly. "This is taking a while to sink in. A *real actual spaceship?*"

"That's right," confirmed Grandpa, nodding his head. "A real actual spaceship. So what do you say?"

Before Bradley could answer, the door slammed open, and Grandma came storming in.

"Grabelon schmabelon!" she roared. "He's going to bed and that's the end of it!"

Bradley groaned.

After a split second of shock, Grandpa sprang to his feet. The joints in his space suit clanked horribly.

"Jemima!" he cried, quickly composing himself. "You look wonderful—wonderful!"

She reached behind her back and tugged uncomfortably at her enormous knickers.

"I do *not*," she growled. "I look like I've been left in someone's pocket and put through the wash. So don't try your charms on me, old man!

Grandpa winked at Bradley. Then he raised his hands and turned to Grandma.

"Jemima!" he began. "My love! How could I *not* try my charms on someone as charming as you? The more charming I find you, the more charming I must be. And then you become more charming still. It's like—heh heh!—*a charms race.*"

She didn't look impressed, so he tried a different tack.

"All I want to do," he told her, taking her hand in both of his own—"All I want to do, my love, is take Bradley on a little trip. Just imagine! An orbit of Saturn! A starlit dash through the asteroids! Surely you remember?"

Her eyes narrowed.

"Go on," she said warily.

"Go on?" cried Grandpa. "Why! Where to begin?"

He gazed deep into her eyes and pressed her hand very fondly. It made a squishy sound, like a glove full of custard.

"A giddy dance by the light of five moons,"

he reminded her breathlessly. "A sweet kiss on a snowy plain, with Jupiter rising in the distance! Holding hands," he finished, "and tumbling together in zero gee—"

"Now hold on a second!" said Bradley. "This isn't the agenda for *our* trip, is it?"

That broke the spell. Grandma snatched her hand back, and something dangerous flashed across her eyes.

"No grandson of mine," she growled, gritting her teeth, "is going off into space with a love rat like you! What kind of example would you set him, womanising your way from planet to planet?"

She stamped her foot, and her shin went *CRACK!*—but she quickly regained her stride.

"And I must say, you've got some cheek—coming back after all these years as if nothing ever happened! Well listen to this! That boy is *not* going into space!"

Grandpa rolled his eyes. Behind his back, he fingered the Brain-O-Matic.

"Then you leave me no choice," he said sadly.

She spotted the strange gadget.

"Oho! So it's *wiping my memory,* is it?" She raised her hands like bony claws, stalking towards him. "Just you wait till I hear about this! I'll be livid!" she promised.

"Jemima, my love, I'm sorry," said Grandpa, backing away—"but the boy deserves a holiday!"

She crouched, ready to attack—but before she could, the Brain-O-Matic came into play. Grandpa thrust it out before him like a crucifix, making her hiss and back away like a vampire. Before she could escape through the door, he gave the top of it a sharp twist.

"Take that, you stupid cow!" he roared.

She gasped—partly at the insult, but also because rays of light were now shooting from her nose and into the Super-Tap. The process looked very painful and made her eyes water. Grandpa held his ground, yanking the tap this way and that while she staggered around and clawed at her face.

There was nothing she could do. As a last resort, she lunged at Grandpa, hoping to scratch his eyes—but before she could, her face went blank, and her arms fell limply by her sides.

At last, Grandpa lowered the device and waved a hand in front of her eyes.

"Jemima?" he muttered.

She didn't react. Her nose began to bleed, giving her a shiny red moustache.

"Well," resumed Grandpa at last—"that's that. She won't remember."

He looked sadly at his old flame. Then he grabbed her shoulders, steered her around and walked her through the door.

"Back in a second," he promised.

"Oh—but wait!" interrupted Bradley, running after him. "I just want to say—I want to come. I absolutely, one hundred percent do."

Grandpa grinned at his new shipmate.

"Glad to hear it!" he said with feeling. "Now wait here."

After a while, he returned alone.

"She's sleeping now," he said, in a sentimental voice.

He produced a white hanky and dabbed his eyes.

"Tremendous woman," he told Bradley. "Absolutely tremendous. She's got guts. I like that—a gal with guts!"

Bradley winced.

"She told me she's prob'ly full of cobwebs," he said uneasily.

Grandpa shrugged.

"Maybe," he agreed. "Funny things, Earthlings. Anyway—I'll be back tomorrow. Expect me at midnight!"

Having said which, he slid the horrible mask onto his face—winked a flashing red eye at Bradley—and flung himself through the open window.

Bradley ran to the window, and saw...

Nothing—not at first; but then he spotted it. A tiny white light, zipping away into nowhere.

Eventually, he shook his head and went back to bed.

LAST DAY ON EARTH

THE NEXT MORNING, Bradley went downstairs and into the kitchen. Dad was in his dressing gown, reaching into a box of cereal.

He saw Bradley and grinned.

"Morning!" he said brightly. "Sorry I was late last night. I got stuck at the office."

His white hair was sticking out in all directions. His glasses, too, were as lopsided as a see-saw. Bradley watched him groping around in the bottom of the box.

"Have we finished all the milk?" he wondered.

Dad shook his head.

"We've got two full bottles," he replied. "The breakfast stuff is on the table."

"Then why are you eating cereal out of the box?"

"I'm not," said Dad simply.

"Right. But you clearly are," noted Bradley—watching as Dad reached into the box again.

Dad just winked, then removed his hand to show a handful of bright orange cheese puffs. He grinned and put them all in his mouth.

Bradley groaned and pinched the bridge of his nose.

"Why are you eating cheese puffs out of a cereal box?" he asked flatly.

Dad held up a finger while he finished chewing, then rolled his eyes and made *Come on, come on!* gestures while he swallowed.

"'Cos we're out of clean bowls!" he said at last. "And the bag split when I was trying to open it. Have you seen Grandma this morning? She isn't very well."

Bradley wandered to the lounge. Grandma was sitting in the armchair, lightly fingering the cotton wool that was stuffed up her nose.

"There's something wrong with my hooter," she complained. "Won't stop bleeding. Hurts like Billy-O!"

He remembered the Brain-O-Matic—which had made hot white light come shooting out of her nostrils—and tried to look surprised.

"How odd," he managed.

Her eyes narrowed. She touched the cotton wool, rubbed her fingers together, and peered at them thoughtfully.

"Yes," she repeated, half to herself. "How odd."

Bradley went to the table, made himself a mug of cornflakes, and began to eat them. After a while, he looked up, and saw that Grandma was eyeballing him suspiciously.

"*Very* odd," she added. "Almost as if—no. Never mind."

He shrugged and returned to his breakfast. She watched him in silence, stroking the fine hairs on her wrinkled chin.

"He came back, didn't he?" she said—quite suddenly.

Bradley half-choked on his cornflakes.

"I beg your pardon?" he squeaked, wiping milk off his chin.

She blinked innocently.

"Doctor Who," she clarified. "They're doing Christmas specials and all sorts. Why? Who did you *think* I meant?"

Bradley rolled his eyes and smiled with relief.

"Oh," he said, spooning cornflakes into his mouth—"I thought you meant Grandpa, that's all."

He dropped his spoon and clapped a hand to his mouth. What a stupid thing to say!

Luckily, Grandma just cupped a shrivelled ear at him.

"What's that?" she barked. "What did you say?"

"I—er—nothing," said Bradley. "Nothing at all," he finished lamely.

After breakfast, Grandma entertained herself by playing with the new stair lift, which had arrived that morning. From the living room, Bradley could watch her head hovering eerily up and down the bannister. Dad locked himself in the study, ostensibly to do some work. However, Bradley could hear the tell-tale

Thwock!—thwock!—thwock! of him playing darts all afternoon.

After a while, Bradley went up to his bedroom and stood by the window, watching the light change on the distant hills. He remembered how he'd found his father in the kitchen, eating cheese puffs from a cereal box with his hair and glasses all crooked. Maybe the old man was starting to go dotty—just like Grandma.

Bradley turned from the window and looked at his action figures, which were arranged on one of the bookshelves.

"We're prob'ly *all* going dotty," he told them glumly. "A break from this place will do me good!"

As the day wore on, his eyelids became very heavy. Eventually, with a last sleepy yawn, he hugged Dad goodnight, coldly shook hands with Grandma, and then went at last to bed, setting his alarm for five minutes to midnight.

(He fell asleep very quickly that night, and only had a single simple dream. He dreamed that he was standing at the window, looking out across the farm. It was a glorious summer evening. The air was filled with fluffy floating seeds, like a net curtain being drawn across the world. In the distance, turning majestically over the grey mountains, was a silver flying saucer, rising and falling softly on the air. Waiting.)

Blast-Off for Bradley!

Beep-beep-beep-beep-beep-beep,   beep-beep-beep-beep-beep-beep-beep-beep-beep-beep-beep,   beep-beep-beep-beep-beep-beep-beep-beep,   beep-beep-beep-beep-beep-beep-beep,   beep-beep,   beep-beep-beep,   beep-beep-beep-beep-beep-beep,   beep-beep-beep-beep-beep-beep-beep-beep-beep,   beep-beep-beep-beep-beep,   beep-beep-beep-beep-beep-beep! went the alarm at five to midnight. Bradley sprang out of bed and rubbed his eyes blankly at the curtains. Through them, he could see a searchlight waving back and forth. A strange humming filled his ears, like the noise of an immense generator.

"What's going on?" he cried, half-asleep still. Then he woke up a little, and shook his head to clear it. Of course—it was Grandpa! In his spaceship!

He scribbled a note for Dad—confessing to the fact that he knew about the Mum situation, and promising to get Grandpa's help on that score—and placed it carefully on the pillow. Then he bit his nails and wondered what to do. He wanted to open the curtains for a proper look. But what if Grandma burst in to stop him leaving?

In the end, instead of wasting any more time, he opened the door, slipped across the landing, and padded softly down the dark, dark stairs.

Halfway down, he paused and had a good hard think about what he was doing. Was it right, just running off without saying a word? Was it enough to leave a note? Shouldn't he at least tell them in person?

But a sudden feeling of resentment welled up inside him, stiffening his resolve.

"Well! There's a lot that no one bothered to tell *me* in person," he reminded himself out loud—"like where Mum was, or Grandpa—so why *should* I tell them? Why *shouldn't* I just run away?"

"Shut up!" called Grandma from her bedroom.

Bradley jumped at the sound of her voice, but then she began to snore. Trying not to wake her again, he tiptoed to the porch. Wild colours flashed through the textured glass. He opened the first door as gently as he could and stepped out onto the cold porch tiles.

He paused, peering anxiously back into the hallway. Would Grandma come droning down the stairs, chasing him on her new stair lift? No, he decided—she was out like a light. She must have been talking in her sleep.

"I can hear you breathing," she snapped bitterly.

He cringed at the sound of her voice, then turned his attention to the front door. His heart began to pound. He held his breath and stretched up on tiptoe, fumbling with the first bolt. It creaked a little as he slid it back, so he paused again, cocking his head to listen.

Nothing.

When he was satisfied, he bent down to undo the second bolt.

This is it, he thought. *Just one more to go.*

As he tugged, the humming sound got louder and louder.

"Come on!" he cried—but it wouldn't budge. He pressed his shoulder to the door and tried again. Nothing! Expecting to be rumbled any second, he put his full weight against the door and unbolted it with a huge *BANG!*

As fast as he could, he opened the door.

And then he gasped.

There it was. Grandpa's flying saucer.

He had never seen anything like it. It whirled overhead like a huge spinning top, making a fierce wind that flattened the grass and sent gravel skipping in all directions. It had a periscope, portholes, and little red lights that raced around the rim.

"Wow!" cried Bradley.

As it hovered over him, a hatch whooshed open like the mouth of a starfish. Circling endlessly around it, made from a matrix of flashing red lights, were the words • • • *EPSILON OMEGA 60+ SERIES* • •.

Bradley covered his face. For a terrifying second, he thought that the huge thing was going to fall on his head. After all—it couldn't *possibly* stay up there.

But it could—and it did.

"Incredible!" cried Bradley.

Suddenly, an extending ladder fell from the hatch, hitting the drive with a muddy C*LUNK!* A spotlight swung towards him, forcing him to cover his eyes. Near the hatch were two brass trumpets that swivelled to face him.

"B*RADLEY!*" cried Grandpa's voice, booming out of them. "I'M ADDRESSING YOU," he explained, "USING ALIEN TECHNOLOGY. THE SOUND OF MY VOICE IS BEING AMPLIFIED BY THE TWO *TRUMPETIZERS*—SAVING ME THE EFFORT," he finished, getting quite hoarse, "OF HAVING TO STRAIN MY VOICE. NOW LISTEN CAREFULLY. I WANT YOU TO ERECT THE LADDER UNDERNEATH THE HATCH."

"Okay, okay!" roared Bradley, running to the ladder. "Keep it down! You'll wake the whole house!"

Moments later, he had the ladder just about

upright. He ran back and forth, trying to poke it through the hatch. The first attempt went horribly wrong. The ladder knocked one of the trumpet things clean off, making it land wetly in the mud.

"You little rascal!" barked Grandpa, sounding only half as loud. "Try again!"

The ladder swung this way and that, teetering like a drunk on stilts. Finally, Grandpa caught the top of it and steered it into the hatch.

"Brilliant!" cried Bradley. He smiled to himself and shot up the ladder. When he reached the top, he looked up, and saw two bright eyes and a white moustache.

Then a pair of arms came down, and pulled him up into the dark interior.

At first, he found himself in near-total darkness.

"Oh—I *am* sorry," said Grandpa suddenly—"I forgot. Your Earthling eyes are useless! Not to worry—I've got some lights."

As he spoke, long white strips began to glow

around them, revealing an enormous egg-like chamber. The walls were white and very smooth, with portholes and a brass rail running around the perimeter.

"It's brilliant!" said Bradley.

Grandpa stood to one side and mopped his face with a hanky. He had pulled the ladder up through the hatch and the effort had taken it out of him.

"Make yourself at home!" he managed at last.

Bradley went to inspect the main console. It had glowing screens, rows of switches, and polished dials with quivering needles.

"Neat," he muttered.

He continued his inspection. On the other side of the console, a green sofa was mounted high on the gleaming white wall. It must have been used a lot, reasoned Bradley, because the silver cushions were squashed right into the corners. There also a bucket nearby, which caught the water that drip, drip, dripped from overhead.

"It's the latest model," resumed Grandpa,

putting the hanky away. "Do you like it?"

Bradley scratched his head.

"I *quite* like it," he began diplomatically. "I just have a few reservations about the leak!"

He pointed at the bucket and grinned awkwardly. Grandpa just rolled his eyes.

"Oh, don't mind that," he told him. "Just a little *hole,* that's all. Luckily, it froze over. Keeps us airtight! But when I re-entered the atmosphere, it started to *thaw.*"

He stopped, seeing that Bradley had gone quite pale.

"Oh, don't worry. It'll soon freeze over again. Once we get into *space,* I mean."

Space! Bradley forgot his fears and shivered with delight. *This is it,* he reminded himself. *I'm inside an actual spaceship!*

He looked around the rest of the cabin, trying to ignore the plop, plop, plopping of water in the bucket. Through the portholes, he could see the dark silhouettes of swaying trees—and behind those, a cloudless sky littered with stars.

"I can't wait to go into space," he said quietly.

Grandpa cracked his knuckles and grinned.

"Then I'd better get started," he said.

First, he emptied the bucket into the round hatch. The globs of water smacked the ground below. Then he removed one of his gloves and clicked his fingers. The eyepiece for a long periscope clattered from the ceiling, dropping down by Bradley's ear. Grandpa strode towards it and stooped to peer through the little lens.

"Well I can see stars," he said at last, "so I suppose we must be pointing in the right direction. Now listen. Before we leave, are you *absolutely sure* you've got everything?"

Bradley was taken aback by that.

"Everything? But I haven't got anything!" he replied.

"Haven't got—? Why!" Grandpa looked surprised. "You're still in your pyjamas! Didn't you pack anything at all? We're going into space! Don't you know what space *is*, Bradley?"

Bradley blushed and scowled furiously.

"Of course I do! But what did you expect? *You've* got a space suit! I *imagined* that you might have one for me!"

But Grandpa had stopped listening. A row of little switches had caught his eye. He paused, frowning at each of them in turn. Then he straightened to read the main screen.

"Never mind," he decided at last. "You can do without a space suit."

Bradley glared at him.

"At the risk of sounding pedantic," he pointed out, "I'm going into space. If I'll *ever* need a space suit, it's prob'ly now!"

Grandpa stared blankly at a rack of levers, then lightly fingered the tops of them.

"Oh, don't worry about that," he assured him. "It's fine—it's fine."

Then he lifted the eyepiece of the periscope, blew into it, and held it to his ear—as if waiting for a reply.

At last, his face brightened.

"*Now* I remember!" he beamed. He strode to the console and gave it a sharp thump. A hatch flipped open, revealing a big red button.

"Look at this!" he said proudly.

Bradley skipped over to see. Circling the button in flashing red lights were the magic words: BLAST-OFF.

Grandpa looked at him, and his eyes twinkled.

"Care to give me a countdown?"

"A what?—oh—five!" breathed Bradley—and suddenly, his skin began to tingle.

"Four!" added Grandpa, putting his mask on.

"Three!" grinned Bradley.

"Two!" cried Grandpa.

"ONE!" roared Bradley, punching the air.

"BLAST-OFF!" they hollered. Grandpa grinned, and slammed his hand on the big red button.

There was an enormous hollow *BANG!*

"Blistering black holes!" bellowed Grandpa— and the ship took off.

Bradley thought he was going to pass out.

As the flying saucer screamed into space, he watched the horizon bend, until the whole world was like a blue-green dish on a starry black table.

"Brilliant!" he roared. Then his legs gave way.

He tumbled backwards, feeling happier than he'd ever felt in his whole life.

After a while, everything calmed down and became very peaceful. Bradley clung to the rim of a porthole, watching the Earth get smaller and smaller.

"Wow," he breathed, shaking his head. "That was unbelievable!"

He turned to Grandpa, who was leaning back with his mask off and his eyes closed, floating around the egg-shaped chamber.

"You're weightless!" gasped Bradley.

Grandpa opened an eye and grinned, doing back-stroke towards the green sofa.

"Of course I am," he laughed. "This is space. There's no gravity in *space*, Bradley."

He reclined serenely on a bed of thin air. A split second later he sat up and frowned.

"I know I asked you this before we took off, but—you *do* know what space is—don't you?"

Bradley scowled.

"I've already told you that I do," he reminded

him. "So stop asking. And anyway—why aren't *I* floating?"

"But you are," replied Grandpa. "Look at your feet."

Bradley did—and saw, to his astonishment, that his toes had risen from the cabin floor, and were now floating quite happily in front of him.

"Help!" he squeaked, rolling drunkenly backwards.

"Calm down!" said Grandpa. "Now listen. Let go of the wall and try swimming around."

"No."

"Honestly. Give it a shot."

Bradley let go with one of his hands. Then, very slowly, he let go with the other. Almost immediately, he pitched to the side and clutched at the wall in a panic.

"Relax!" urged Grandpa from the sofa. He'd found a newspaper and a pair of reading glasses and was looking at the sports pages. "Just give the wall a good, hard kick and see what happens."

"All right, all right!" muttered Bradley. "Give

me chance!"

There was nothing for it. He shut his eyes—pointed his head at Grandpa—and kicked the wall with both feet.

There was a sensation of falling. Seconds later, Grandpa had him by the ankle.

"There you go!" he beamed, plonking him down on the sofa.

Bradley clutched the edge of the seat with both hands. He had turned quite pale, but Grandpa just laughed at him.

"Don't worry," he assured him. "You won't fly off. The sofa has its own gravity, you see—so unless you jump off it, you'll stay where you are."

He pointed to a little logo on the arm of the chair.

"Designed by 'Gravitational' Len Zing. He does artificial gravity. Cost a fortune."

Bradley let go. He stayed where he was, and a nervous grin spread across his face.

"I could get used to this!" he decided, putting his hands behind his head. "Reckon I'll stay here for a bit—with the gravity."

"Sounds reasonable to me!" beamed Grandpa.

Then, without warning, he grabbed Bradley by the back of his collar and threw him at the ceiling.

Bradley was furious.

"What are you doing?!" he roared. He hit the wall and shot up it like a pinball.

"You'll thank me later," promised Grandpa. "Now practise."

Having said which, he began to retrieve the loose pages of his paper. These had come apart in his hands, and now, flapping lazily like great white water birds, were migrating weightlessly across the cabin.

Bradley realised that he was stuck on the ceiling.

"Grandpa?" he said unhappily.

Grandpa didn't look up.

"Practise!" he insisted.

After a while, Grandpa abandoned his attempts to put the paper back together. Instead, he kicked himself to the console, explaining that he needed to chart a course to the end of the Solar System. A hologram appeared in the centre of the cabin. He held a protractor in front of it, trying to measure the angle of the ship's trajectory. As he did, the loose newspaper pages gathered overhead, roosting lightly in the centre of the ceiling.

Bradley span around, flapping his arms and looking silly. It took half an hour to get back to the sofa, but it was good practice—and hilarious to watch, according to Grandpa—especially when he collided with the floor and span like a bottle, crossing his arms and sulking furiously.

"It's all part of the learning curve," said Grandpa brightly. "I tell you what though. By the time you get to Grabelon, you'll be an old pro!"

STAR-PUPS AND FIZZY POP

THE FIRST LEG of the cruise was an exciting time for Bradley. Every now and then, Grandpa would fetch meals in foil bags with little nozzles. These tasted like baby food, but squeezing them out was a fun novelty. After a while, Bradley even got used to being weightless, and mastered the art of kicking himself off the walls and ceiling.

Sleeping in zero gee was truly remarkable too. When night came, Grandpa would dim the tubes that arched across the chamber, and the two of them would fall into a deep, weightless sleep filled with strange starry dreams.

The first leg was also a very *bizarre* time for Bradley. For instance—midway through the first day, Grandpa drew his attention to a silver dome on a glowing plastic pedestal.

"Look at this," he told him. "Open up!" he added brightly, knocking on the dome.

It creaked open to reveal a bubble of thick glass. Inside it was a *human brain,* with bubbles clinging to its wrinkled surface. Bradley swam over to see. At the front of the brain, sticking out between a pair of furrowed grey lobes, was—a great big nose!

"It's got a nose," he observed stupidly.

"That's right!" agreed Grandpa, clapping a hand on his shoulder. "A great big nose. This is Captain Nosegay. He helps me navigate in deep space. Do you see?"

He pointed to a rope of cables, which linked the base of the pedestal to the console.

"He has a highly sensitive nose," explained Grandpa. "Smells radio waves—stuff like that."

Having said which, he clicked his fingers, and the dome snapped shut again.

On the second day, Grandpa beckoned Bradley to a porthole. Captain Nosegay's dome had opened, and he was listing an endless series of numbers in a robotic voice.

"What's he doing?" wondered Bradley.

"He's spotted Mars," explained Grandpa. "Look."

Bradley pressed his face to the porthole. Mars was round and red like a terracotta ashtray. It was hardly more exciting than the moon on a clear night.

"Is that it?" he wondered.

Grandpa bristled.

"Well give it chance!" he muttered. "Here, let me show you."

He went to the controls, cranked a few of the levers, and brought them swooping down across the dusty Martian plain. It was a desolate world, cracked and dry, littered with enormous red rocks.

Suddenly, Bradley saw something in the distance and gasped.

"Pyramids!" he cried.

As they raced towards them, he saw that each was made from sullen dark stone, with a sinister slit window staring from the top.

"That's right," agreed Grandpa. "Pyramids! And if you think *those* are good," he promised, with a sudden sparkle in his eyes, "then wait till we get to the city!"

"What city?" wondered Bradley.

"The Holy City," clarified Grandpa, grinning darkly over the controls, "of the *Dessicat.*"

Twenty minutes later, as they soared above the parched remains of old canals, Grandpa slowed down. Bradley pressed his face to the porthole. Here and there, the skeletons of long wooden barges lay abandoned in the dust. After a while, the ground began to rise towards a distant jagged peak.

"Olympus Mons," announced Grandpa.

Bradley ignored him. He was thinking of the barges. Barges—on the surface of another planet! How had they gone unnoticed? Had NASA's rovers gone roving in the wrong direction, he wondered?

"I thought this was a *dead* world," he muttered, half to himself.

"Well, as you can see, it's hardly thriving,"

agreed Grandpa—"but 'dead' is a bit strong. Ah! Here we are."

At long last, they crowned the ancient peak of Olympus Mons. Far below them, beginning in the barren foothills, were the outskirts of a sprawling stone city. The Holy City was red, like the rest of Mars, with dusty domes and rocky towers. It looked deserted—a ghost town—but here and there, a wavering light would flicker in a window. Faraway, in a great dusty courtyard, Bradley could see the giant red statue of a cat.

"This," announced Grandpa, wheeling gracefully around it, "is the Dessicat—a strange and very vengeful god! The Martians worship it and hate it at the same time. They believe that it drank all the water and turned Mars into a desert."

Bradley stared through his little porthole. The Dessicat was enormous, with blank, baleful eyes that gazed deep into the secret sadness of a desert world.

"But why would you worship something like

that?" he wondered out loud.

Grandpa just shrugged.

"Who knows? Appeasement? The Martians have only so much water left," he explained, "and they're desperately trying to keep it. It's a strange religion."

Having said which, he cranked another lever and the saucer roared off into the red sky. Bradley was thrown briefly against the floor.

"There's a lot of strange things in the universe," continued Grandpa. "Dangerous things, too—like *pirates*," he finished darkly.

Bradley said nothing. He just stayed by the window, watching the red horizon close in on itself. It curved and became a complete circle. He pressed his face to the glass, thinking of the Martians—those poor, thirsty creatures, cowering in the shadow of their cruel Dessicat.

"Huh. *Pirates!*" said Grandpa again.

His hand rose automatically to his neck, seeming to feel for something that wasn't there.

"You don't want to meet those guys," he muttered.

Later that day, while the eerie red world was shrinking from sight, Grandpa spotted something that made his face light up.

"Star-pups!" he cried, punching the air. "A whole shoal of 'em! Come and look!"

Bradley dropped his supper and floated over. Outside, the most incredible creatures were falling through space like enormous snowflakes. They had no arms or legs, and reminded him of pompoms, or huge balls of fluff—except that, scrunched up in the middle of their round bodies, they had tiny little faces and long white whiskers. They glowed strangely in the darkness, like weird fish from the bottom of the ocean.

"Star-pups?" echoed Bradley.

They were all different colours. Neon pink, day-glo yellow, glow-in-the-dark green. The smallest were the size of scotch eggs, and one or two were bigger than basketballs.

"I don't get it," said Bradley. "How do they live out there?"

"They absorb most of their energy from starlight," explained Grandpa—joining Bradley at the porthole—"and eat pretty much anything they come across. Rocks, ice, space junk—you name it."

Bradley continued to gaze at the star-pups. Every single one of them looked worried. He guessed it had something to do with the fact that they were falling through space.

"They're brilliant," he decided. "They look worried though, don't they?"

"They do," agreed Grandpa.

Then something occurred to him, and his face lit up.

"Why don't you wait here while I try to catch one?" he suggested. "I tell you what though— you might want to hold on to something when the hatch opens!"

Bradley found the brass rail and gripped it with both hands. As he did, Grandpa got a butterfly net and some kind of hose from the storage cupboard.

"Air supply," he explained—fitting the hose to

his mask. Then he floated to the centre of the cabin.

"Any minute now," he promised.

Nothing happened.

"Well?" said Bradley after a while.

Before Grandpa could reply, the round hatch opened, and he was blown out into space.

In a flash, Bradley felt very cold. The cabin became very windy. His feet were pulled towards the hatch by a fierce sucking draft, and the sight of the naked stars through the opening made him shiver. He gripped the rail so hard that his knuckles turned white.

Then the unthinkable happened.

His pyjama bottoms began to come off!

Suddenly, he could feel the cold air on his naked bum. It was as if a powerful vacuum cleaner had caught the bottom of his pyjamas. He wriggled this way and that, praying that there weren't any deadly cosmic rays zapping his exposed behind through the open hatch.

"Grandpa!" he cried. "Close the hatch! It's wide open!"

The ends of his pyjama bottoms now covered his feet, flapping loudly in the wind. He imagined the soft *zipping* sound they would make if they came off entirely and shot into space.

There was nothing for it. He let go of the rail with one hand in order to grab at the bottoms. With the other, he continued to cling desperately to the brass rail.

Which—quite suddenly—came loose from the wall.

Bradley screamed as he, the rail, and lots of little screws shot towards the hatch.

"Grandpa!" he cried. "Help me!"

Luckily, before he was blown into space, the hatch closed, making a seal around the line for Grandpa's air supply. The screws hit the inside of it a split-second later, bouncing loudly like machine gun rounds.

Bradley cannonballed the cabin floor, bounced off it, and rose weightlessly into the air. He hovered by the pedestal, half-stunned by the ordeal—clinging to the rail like a bit of driftwood. Then he straightened his pyjama bottoms, threw the rail grumpily into the storage cupboard, and went to a porthole.

Moments later, Grandpa tumbled into view, swinging his butterfly net this way and that. Bradley cursed him through the porthole, forgetting that sound can't travel through a vacuum.

"You idiot!" he cried, thumping the glass. "I nearly died!"

Grandpa couldn't hear him. Either way, he was busy trying to catch a star-pup. He swung his net at the falling creatures, batting them left and right by accident, until—at long last—he managed to catch an enormous white one. He gave Bradley the thumbs-up and hauled himself back to the spaceship.

Bradley grabbed Captain Nosegay's pedestal and stared impatiently at the round hatch. Quite suddenly, it whooshed open. Everything became windy again. A spidery gloved hand crawled into sight, groping for a handhold. Then Grandpa's mask popped into view, followed by the tip of the butterfly net.

"Blistering black holes!" he muttered.

He climbed through the whistling hatch and tried to swim away from it, pumping his legs like a huge frog. Then the hatch closed and the roaring wind died in an instant. Satisfied that he was safe, Bradley let go of the pedestal.

"Phew!" sighed Grandpa, getting his breath back. "That reminds me—I really *must* install some sort of airlock!"

"Yes!" said Bradley testily. "You must!"

Grandpa removed his mask, squeezed the sweat from his moustache, and shook the star-pup from the bottom of the net. It glided slowly away from him, seeming just as worried as it had when it had been outside.

Bradley forgot all about his ordeal. He was face-to-face with an *actual real alien.* He kicked himself over and reached out to stroke it. As he did, he gasped at the icy softness of the creature's fur. He ran his hand deep into the fine white hair, trying to picture what sort of body was underneath it—but there didn't seem to *be* a body. In fact, it seemed to be nothing but fur. He continued to stroke it while Grandpa screwed the rail back onto the wall.

Eventually, the old astronaut went to the sofa and started putting his newspaper back together. Bradley sat down beside him, watching the strange creature as it explored the cabin.

"Why pick a big one?" he wondered. The star-pup stopped by the periscope, sniffed the green eyepiece, and rubbed along it like a cat. "The small ones are cuter, I think. But this one's still pretty good," he finished blandly.

Grandpa glanced up.

"It's all about *timing*," he replied. "This one is about to give birth—any minute now!"

He checked his watch.

"Any minute now," he repeated firmly, as if giving an actor his cue.

The star-pup drifted to the console and went briefly into orbit around it. Then it sailed off backwards and bumped into the wall, squeaking sadly to itself. Grandpa flapped the paper and cleared his throat pointedly.

"Any—minute—now!" he insisted.

Bradley, meanwhile, was delighted.

"Give birth?" he echoed. "What—to a baby star-pup?"

But Grandpa shook his head.

"More than one," he warned—and he looked a little scared behind the huge paper.

About five minutes later, it happened. The star-pup paused by the periscope, opened its little mouth, and began suddenly to sing. Bradley was so surprised that he nearly jumped out of his skin.

"Why's it doing that?" he wondered.

Grandpa grabbed his arm.

"Be quiet!" he hissed. "This is it! It's beginning!"

Bradley sat and listened. There were no words, as such—just long, eerie notes that rose and fell, making the hairs rise on the back of his neck.

"Aha!" observed Grandpa. "Here we go!"

It took Bradley a second to see what was

different. Then it clicked. The star-pup *didn't look worried any more.* It looked relieved.

At last, the strange little creature fell silent. It smiled the small serene smile of one who had finally found peace.

Pop! it went—filling the cabin with baby star-pups.

Bradley gasped. There were hundreds of them, all different colours, flying away in all directions. They were no bigger than golf balls and all looked worried, whizzing around and bouncing off the walls.

He laughed with surprise. Then he jumped up from the sofa and did backstroke through the middle of them.

Grandpa just grinned.

"Great things, star-pups," he said as they fussed over Bradley. "I wonder what it is that troubles them so? Either way—whatever it is, they work it out in the end. And then they explode. Brilliant!"

He shook his head and laughed, and Bradley laughed with him.

* * *

The next day, Grandpa announced that the star-pups had to go—"or they'll eat the monitors," he explained nervously. Bradley held on while the hatch opened, blowing them all into space—all except for one, which he clutched in his free hand. It was a snow-white one, which Grandpa was letting him keep as a pet. Bradley had christened him Waldo, and had spent the whole morning feeding him rubbish and chasing him away from the instruments.

Later that morning, Grandpa announced that they were near the Asteroid Belt and would go *shopping* there the next day. Waldo greeted the news with a worried look. Bradley wasn't fazed by that. He understood that Waldo would *always* look worried, until the time came at last for him to sing his strange little song and explode in a shower of babies. That, it seemed, was the life cycle of the star-pups.

But this time, Bradley was also worried.

"Won't I need a space suit to leave the ship?"

Grandpa shook his head.

"It's got an atmosphere," he promised. "The whole belt. And the asteroids have gravity, so you can walk around them quite comfortably. Some of them are so close together that you can jump the gap, or swing across on ropes. It used to be a planet called Phaeton, but it blew up."

Bradley shot him a funny look.

"I'm pretty sure that *none* of what you just said is true," he said. "I've got a book about space. The Asteroid Belt is mostly empty. It certainly doesn't have an atmosphere and it wasn't a planet."

But Grandpa just smiled, and said, "You'd be surprised how little you Earthlings know!"

Later that day, as they made their way towards the Asteroid Belt, Grandpa brought out a treat: a rocket-shaped bottle of fizzy pop.

"Gee Whiz Soda," he announced happily. "Artificial gravity for less than a calorie! Fancy trying it?"

Bradley swam over to see. The label was made of holographic foil and had the words *Gee Whiz Soda* swirling across it in bubbly black handwriting. Grandpa held the bottle to the light, and Bradley saw that it was the colour (or rather colours) of petrol on water—dark and dangerous.

"What is it?" he wondered.

Grandpa unscrewed the lid.

"It's a popular gravity drink," he explained. "Watch!"

He took a big swig. Before he could wipe his mouth, he dropped suddenly downwards, landing feet-first on the cabin floor. The sudden jolt caused a few frothy drops to spill from the bottle, and they formed weightless globs overhead.

"What happened?" wondered Bradley.

Grandpa grinned stupidly, shifting his weight from foot to foot, and took a few steps backwards. It looked very strange to Bradley, who was finally used to things floating around.

"I don't get it," he said. "How does it work?"

But Grandpa just offered him the bottle.

"Try it," he insisted.

Bradley shrugged and took it. Then, somersaulting slowly overhead, he took a swig. He expected to join Grandpa on the floor, but because he was upside-down to begin with, he fell in the opposite direction, and flew feet-first towards the ceiling.

He landed overhead in a clumsy heap. Suddenly, because he'd been weightless for so long, he felt very heavy.

He frowned and licked his lips.

"Mm. Tastes like *cream soda,*" he observed. "What's it for?"

Grandpa looked up at him.

"It's a gravity drink," he explained. "Artificial gravity for less than a calorie. Does exactly what it says on the bottle!"

Bradley tried to walk down the wall, thinking that he could join Grandpa on the floor—but apparently, that wasn't going to work. Whenever he got halfway there, he lost his footing and slid back up.

"It's no good," Grandpa told him. "You were upside down when you drank it—so for you, the ceiling is the floor."

Bradley ignored him and kept trying. Finally, he settled in the centre of the ceiling, crossed his arms, and pulled a face.

"Why didn't you tell me about this before?" he complained. "It took me *ages* to get used to floating around."

"I didn't tell you because floating around is half the fun," replied Grandpa. "Otherwise, why leave Earth in the first place? And besides," he joked—"it—heh heh!—it *makes you put on weight.*"

Before long, the effects began to fade. Soon, Bradley found that he could run right down the walls, floating back up only when he reached the floor.

"Nearly!" he'd mutter.

After just a few minutes, he and Grandpa were weightless again, floating around the egg-shaped cabin. To his surprise, Bradley found the he was relieved.

"Strange," he observed—pushing himself lightly into the centre of the cabin. He span slowly like a puck on ice. "I think I'm getting the hang of this!"

Grandpa nodded.

"You are," he agreed. "You'll make a sterling astronaut yet!"

That night, when they turned off the lights and fell into their deep, weightless sleep, Bradley dreamed of Earth. He dreamed of bright winter evenings and windswept trees. He dreamed of hanging baskets dripping water. He dreamed of his deserted fair rusting in the long grass—the tombola turning wetly in the wind.

After a while, he began to dream of clicking needles, dark hatches, and icy coffins. He dreamed of Grandma, pacing up and down on the landing. She looked lost, as if she had come upstairs and forgotten why. It was something that she did in real life, and Bradley guessed that it had something to do with getting old. The look on her face reminded him of the star-pups. He wondered if she would explode in a cloud of tiny Grandmas—but she didn't. She just went on looking worried, and made her way to the bathroom.

Bradley woke up feeling troubled. He blinked, rubbing his eyes. For the first time, he felt sad about being in space. How was everyone back home, he wondered? Running away, he decided, had actually been pretty selfish. He gazed through a porthole, wondering what would happen when he went back home.

Home. There it was, he suddenly realised—a blue-green star glowing brightly in the darkness.

He rolled over and looked at Grandpa.

"Are you going to bring Mum back to life?" he asked. "When we go home, I mean?"—but Grandpa just snored and smacked his lips.

Bradley wasn't awake for long. The minute he closed his eyes, he began to nod off. Soon, he was flying through a universe of his own—dreaming of parrots roosting in the rings of Saturn, and other impossible things.

A SPACE SUIT FOR BRADLEY

THE NEXT MORNING, when Bradley woke up, he went straight to the porthole and pressed his nose to the glass. The Asteroid Belt had appeared overnight. It was a brilliant shaft of clear blue light that arched across the darkness, filled with dancing dust motes. It dawned on Bradley that the tiny bright specks were probably the asteroids. It was nothing like the picture in his book.

"It's glowing," he said at last—shielding his eyes.

"That's because of sunlight hitting the atmosphere," called Grandpa from the console. "I *did* tell you, didn't I? Anyway—you stay there while I take us in."

Bradley watched the belt draw closer and

closer, until the bright blue glare made it hard to see. Grandpa steered the ship until they were right on top of it. It shone ahead of them like a blue neon river that flowed into darkness.

At last, Bradley's eyes adjusted to the light. Through the glare, he began to make out the asteroids themselves. They rolled through the light below, colliding silently and breaking into identical smaller pieces.

Suddenly, Bradley noticed something very strange. One of the asteroids had a *tree* growing out of it. The tree was three times taller than the asteroid itself and dangled ripe blue fruit from its branches. Wet roots sprouted from the bottom of the asteroid, curling away into space.

"I didn't know there were *trees* out here," he muttered.

"Of course there are," replied Grandpa. "Why wouldn't there be? Now let me concentrate."

Bradley left him to it. Soon after, a magnificent forest floated into view. The treetops jostled wetly and lianas snaked weightlessly between them.

Suddenly, through a gap in the green canopy, he spotted a young girl with a pretty red dress and a jet pack. She moved from branch to branch, picking the fruit and filling a basket. Eventually, she spotted Bradley and waved. He blushed and waved back, then lost sight of her in the dense forest.

Then he saw a big flat asteroid with what seemed to be a shop on it. The shop had space suits hanging in the windows, and (Bradley rubbed his eyes) an empty car park in front of it. The sign above the door read, "Wuztop Nash, Gentlemen's Tailors—New York, Paris, An Asteroid. Now Open." Beneath that, someone had added, "Parking for Patrons Only."

"I know you said you wanted a space suit," explained Grandpa, as the ship swooped down to land—"so I guess we ought to get you one!"

"What—honestly? A space suit?"

Bradley grinned with delight, then returned his gaze to the approaching asteroid. As the spaceship hovered closer and closer to the car park, Grandpa pulled out a wallet and looked inside it.

"Just checking I've got some *winnies*," he explained. "Most of the shops in the Asteroid Belt only accept winnies."

The wallet looked very full. Grandpa pulled out a wad of notes, showing Bradley the foil holograms and weird designs. Then he dug his thumb and forefinger into the zip-up pouch and found a shiny new winnie for Bradley to have.

Bradley held it in his palm and peered down at it. It was shaped like a square and was the colour of a five pence piece, with a design showing rocks and smiling faces tumbling along a wavy line.

"Properly speaking, the plural of winnie is wince," explained Grandpa—"but it's quite old fashioned to say so. Instead of ten wince, most people would say, *ten wee*."

Bradley turned it over. The tails side of the coin read, *Issued by the Iapetus Mint for the Commonwealth of Worlds and Micro-Worlds Formerly Comprising the Planet Phaeton.*

He thanked Grandpa and dropped the coin into his pyjama breast pocket.

"Are there lots of different currencies in space?" he asked—hoping that Grandpa would take the hint and give him some more. "Different types, I mean? Only I suppose I could start a collection, couldn't I?"

"Oh, yes," confirmed Grandpa. "There's even more than one for the Asteroid Belt. One asteroid not far from here uses the *pic.*"

"Well have you got any pics?"

Grandpa shook his head.

"*The* pic," he repeated. "Everyone's pretty poor there. It's worth about twenty pee, but they're all too scared to spend it."

Eventually, Bradley and Grandpa dropped out of the circular hatch and landed on the tarmac below. There were lines painted on the car park, dividing it into different parking spaces, and Grandpa had parked the spaceship rather badly.

"Oh well," he decided. He hovered,

wondering whether or not to re-park it, then shrugged and strolled towards the shop.

"Come along!" he sang impatiently.

Bradley ran after him. As he did, a very small asteroid whistled overhead, making him cringe with fright. It bounced between the larger rocks like a pinball, disappearing down the crowded belt.

Waldo looked very worried by all this. Before they left the saucer, Grandpa had found a bit of old string for Bradley to use as a lead. One end was looped around Waldo and the other was tied to Bradley's wrist. He gave it a tug and hurried after Grandpa, ducking again as another tiny asteroid sailed overhead.

They reached the shop and bumbled through the door. A little bell went *DING!* and a man with powder-blue skin sprang out from behind the counter—armed (Bradley was alarmed to see) with some kind of long grey laser rifle.

"Hello sirs!" he said brightly, placing it on the counter before him. "Wuztop Nash, gentlemen's tailor. Are you looking to buy a suit? Or," he added darkly—letting his hand fall lightly on the gun—"just browsing?"

Grandpa looked down at the gun.

"Browsing? Certainly not," he assured him coldly. "I need a space suit for my young apprentice. What have you got?"

Wuztop turned to Bradley. The minute he saw him, his face froze.

"What in blue blazes is this?" he wondered. "Pyjamas—in space? What were you thinking?"

He turned to Grandpa, and said behind his hand—"This young man—why is he wearing pyjamas?"

"I don't know," replied Grandpa unhappily. "I told him we were going into space, and *that's* what he turned up in!"

"Well doesn't he know what space is?"

Bradley stamped his foot suddenly.

"I know *perfectly well* what space is," he assured them coldly. "Look. It's *space*, okay? It's the *space* between planets." He began to count off the features of space on his fingers. "There isn't any *oxygen*. You're *weightless*.

There isn't any *up or down*."

Grandpa and Wuztop shared a worried glance.

"Well of *course* there's an up and down," said Grandpa gently. "Look lad—there's one of them, right there."

He was jerking a thumb at the ceiling. Then Wuztop pointed to the floor.

"And that one's down," he added helpfully.

Bradley grabbed his hair in both hands and cried out in frustration. Then he glared at the pair of them.

"Either way," he growled at last—"I'm wearing *pyjamas* because I wasn't aware that *space* had a *dress code* and no one thought to tell me otherwise!"

The tailor looked stunned by Bradley's outburst.

"Okay, okay! Calm down!" he said. He reached behind the counter for his tape measure. "Either way," he added over his shoulder—"you've come to the right place. If *anyone* can make a silk purse out of a space cow's ear, it's Wuztop Nash!"

When he straightened with his tape measure, he saw that Bradley had stormed off in a sulk.

"Hey! You won't fit into *that*," he called after him.

He made this last remark because Bradley had gone off across the shop floor to see some space suits that clearly weren't for humans. As well as brass suits and white suits and suits like tin foil, there were suits with no legs or six arms or pointed gloves for the tips of tentacles. There were suits with two heads, no heads, transparent visors on stalks, and even one that was the shape of a cello.

Specifically, Bradley had stopped to inspect a small round one on a pedestal. It looked like a tiny diving bell, with a little round porthole at the front.

"You won't fit into *that*," repeated Wuztop. "It's for star-pups."

Bradley looked at it and pulled a face.

"But why?" he wondered—coming out from behind the pedestal. "They don't *need* space suits."

Wuztop looked disgusted.

"Fashion," he announced primly, "has *nothing* to do with what is *needed*. Fashion only cares about what is *now*. Why—this very minute, fashionistas from the ice plains of Sedna are walking out in shades and Bermuda shorts! It is very cold there. Some of them will die. But *none* of them will look unfashionable. Now come here," he told Bradley, holding out the tape measure, "and let me make you over."

Bradley stood patiently while the strange blue tailor fussed around him, measuring his chest, his waist, his inside leg and the length of each arm. Lastly, Wuztop measured his fingers and got out a glossy catalogue, which had pages and pages showing different kinds of hands from all over the Solar System.

"How many fingers was it again?"

"Four," said Bradley. "Four fingers and one thumb."

"Right." Wuztop frowned and flipped through the pages. "And which hand was the thumb on again...?"

At long last, the tailor was very nearly ready to make Bradley's space suit.

"White plastic, black rubber, or silver foil?" he asked, rubbing his hands eagerly.

Bradley thought about it.

"Silver," he decided. Grandpa groaned in the background.

"I see, I see." Wuztop made a note of that. "And what about the eyes? Flashing lights, or little windows?"

"Windows—like portholes, please."

"Perfect," agreed Wuztop—writing it down. "Portholes are very *in* this season. Portholes and heels. Would you like a cute pair of heels, Bradley?"

Bradley turned pale.

"I hardly think I need *high heels*," he muttered.

"Oh—not *high* high heels. About an inch. They'd make you look like a cowboy—from space!"

Bradley started to warm to the idea, but Grandpa wasn't happy.

"No high heels!" he growled from the corner.

The tailor glared at him.

"Very well. I'll be five seconds," he promised.

He ducked behind the counter and emerged moments later with a full space suit.

"That was quick," muttered Bradley.

The tailor looked annoyed.

"Everything's hand-made to order," he insisted—as if Bradley had meant to imply that it wasn't. Then he took Bradley by the shoulders and steered him to the fitting rooms.

A short while later, Bradley was able to admire his new space suit in the mirror. It was perfect—like a suit of futuristic armour. He stood side-on and puffed his chest out.

"Brilliant," he said at last.

Then he rose lightly on the tips of his toes, watching the silver boots change shape.

"Maybe I should have got the cowboy heels after all," he muttered.

Eventually, Grandpa poked his head through the curtains and whistled.

"Very smart!" he beamed. "Now take it off so we can pay for it."

Bradley's shoulders fell.

"Can't I wear it out?" he groaned.

But Grandpa shook his head.

"You can wear it later," he promised. "Chop chop!"

Bradley scowled as he took off the suit and put on his pyjamas. Moments later, the tailor put it in a bag and began to count out a fat wad of Grandpa's money. The odd-looking till went DING, opened with a strange glugging sound, and sucked up the notes like a little black hole.

Grandpa saw Bradley sulking in the corner.

"You can wear it later," he promised. "Just wait till we're back on the saucer."

Bradley cheered up at that. As they left the shop, Grandpa inspected the contents of his wallet, looking slightly anxious as they strolled back to the saucer—but he cheered up too when he saw how happy Bradley was.

"That's the spirit!" he said warmly.

The tailor came to the door and waved them

off with his laser rifle. Everyone was happy except for Waldo, who trailed behind them on his bit of string looking confused and miserable.

"Bye!" called Wuztop from the doorway. He closed one eye and pretended to sight them down the barrel of the gun. "Pow pow! Ha ha! Come again soon!" he added hopefully.

Grandpa turned to wave.

"It's a funny place, the Solar System," he said wistfully. "But you're learning that all by yourself, I'm sure."

When they got back to the spaceship, Bradley pounced on the carrier bag. He was all set to change into his new space suit—but before he could, Grandpa confiscated the bag and held it out of reach.

"Save it for Grabelon," he said firmly. "You want to look *nice and smart* for Grabelon, don't you?"

Bradley tried to grab it.

"What? *Save* it? But you promised I could wear it now!"

Grandpa held the bag high above his head.

"Mm? Well yes," he conceded at last—pulling a face as if he might relent. "I suppose I *did* promise. Didn't I?"

Then he grinned and snapped his fingers.

"Ha ha!" he cried. "Ho ho! A ruse, Bradley—a mere ruse!" And he took the bag triumphantly to the cupboard and left it there.

After that, Bradley sat sulking in his old pyjamas, pulling at the sleeves in disgust. Still chuckling to himself, Grandpa piloted the saucer down the Asteroid Belt, zigzagging from rock to rock.

"A mere ruse!" he repeated happily. "I tell you what, Bradley—isn't it great to be flying through space? The sun behind us—the Solar Wind streaming through our hair—and to top it all, we're wearing some really spiffing space suits! Oh, I'm sorry, I completely forgot. *You're* in pyjamas. Ha ha! What a card!"

Bradley just scowled.

"These asteroids," added Grandpa eventually—"reminds me of the time I was attacked by *pirates*. I was orbiting Mars when they appeared out of nowhere. *Cloaking* device, you see. Straight away, they tried to board me, so I hot-footed it to the Asteroid Belt and knocked against the rocks to scrape 'em off. They're like limpets, you see. One actually forced the hatch and got inside—a great big one, with a jagged scar between his big blank eyes!"

Bradley forgot that he was meant to be in a bad mood and floated over.

"What happened?" he wondered.

"Well, I was younger back then," shrugged Grandpa, "and much fitter. I'd be in real trouble if it happened now! Anyway, we fought hand to hand—him with his horrible grey paws—me with my right hook! I managed to beat him back, but before he was blown into space, he reached out and tore a silver locket from around my neck. It was very dear to me. Not expensive. But dear, all the same."

They continued down the asteroid belt, seeing more and more strange sights. They saw open-topped spaceships, with space fishermen loading bait and rods onto the backs of them. In the distance, Bradley could see them casting their long lines deep into space, with flashing lures at the end of them.

Then there was nothing to see for a while except the cratered white rubble of the asteroids. At last, they got out at a very small asteroid with an ice cream hut and two round tables. One of the tables was already occupied by a pretty girl of about Bradley's age. She perched on her little stool, licking chocolate sprinkles off the back of a spoon.

"Hello!" she said brightly. Bradley blushed and refused to look at her.

Meanwhile, at the ice cream stand, Grandpa ordered chocolate for Bradley and vanilla for himself. He asked for all the toppings, muttering, "A few more, perhaps—that's the ticket!"—until his cone and the counter were covered in crushed nuts.

"Just ah—just a few more," he repeated, staring hopefully at the sticky mess.

The ice cream man glared and held out his hand for payment.

After that, Bradley and Grandpa sat themselves down and chatted about the second leg of the journey. Grandpa warned that it would take a day or two to reach Grabelon, but promised a flyby of Saturn on the way there.

Bradley frowned.

"Saturn? Isn't it Jupiter first?" he wondered.

Grandpa looked at him as if he were a complete idiot.

"They're not in a *straight line,* are they?" he pointed out. "Jupiter's closer to the sun, all right, but it's currently on the other side of it. Anyway—it's a whole day as the crow flies— provided the crow had a spaceship like ours, of course—but if we zigzag a bit, we can pick up Saturn and Pluto."

Bradley didn't mind how long it took. It was very peaceful, sitting out there on the little asteroid. As they enjoyed their ice creams, the saucer turned majestically overhead like a parasol.

After a while, Bradley glanced at the girl—and saw, to his surprise, that she was glancing back at him. She seemed completely human, except for the fact that (he suddenly realised, with a horrible sinking sensation) she *only had one eye.*

He looked away. Only one eye? He picked up his spoon, angled it to catch her reflection, and did a quick recount. His heart sank. No matter how he angled the spoon, he could only see one eye in the back of it. It wasn't bang in the middle, like a cyclops, or anywhere silly like stuck on her chin. Her one eye was perfectly normal. She just didn't have the other one.

Suddenly, her reflection seemed to stare right at him. He dropped the spoon in fright—then, feeling suddenly self-conscious, retrieved it and started wolfing down his ice cream for the sake of having something to do.

He could feel her one horrible eye still watching him as he shovelled it into his mouth. Then the inevitable happened and he got an ice cream headache. The pain mounted to an astonishing crescendo as he closed his eyes and squeezed the bridge of his nose.

"Are you all right?" asked Grandpa.

"Stand aside!" roared a small voice. "This boy is choking!"

Suddenly, with surprising strength, the one-eyed girl leapt out from behind her table, pulled Bradley off his stool, and started giving him the Heimlich manoeuvre. The shock of being hoisted upright and thrown around made him inhale a mouthful of cold ice cream and cough it up again.

"My word," gasped Grandpa. "You're right— he *is* choking!"

"Don't worry," said the girl coolly—"I've got it under control!"

After a while, Bradley got his breath back and managed to extract himself from the one-eyed girl. He glared at her, but Grandpa was thoroughly impressed.

"Young lady," he said in a wavering voice—"my grandson owes you his life. When your parents get here, I'll be sure to tell them so."

She had been trying to get Bradley on the ground so that she could put him in the recovery position, but at the mention of *parents* she stopped and looked up.

"Parents? Oh, I don't have any. I'm from Pluto. We grow in the ground—like plants!"

Grandpa looked impressed.

"Remarkable!" he said to her. "Well I've *heard* of the one-eyed pod-people of Pluto, but I must say, you're the first one I've ever actually met. How did you get here, all by yourself?"

"I hitched a lift with some paramedics," she explained. "They taught me the basics, and now I do freelance work in return for ice cream. Business is slow, but the guy in the hut gets panic attacks and hyperventilates, so it's regular at least."

Grandpa checked his wallet and looked embarrassed.

"I see," he said. "Well normally, I'd buy you a *great big bowl* of ice cream—but I'm having a bit of a cash flow crisis. Apparently, only a *silver* space suit is good enough for *little Lord*

Fauntleroy here," he finished bitterly.

Bradley glared at the table and said nothing.

"But never mind," continued Grandpa. "This is Bradley, and I'm Grandpa. Who are you?"

"Headlice," replied the girl—blinking prettily with her one blue eye.

Grandpa looked delighted.

"Headlice!" he cooed. "Why—what a pretty name! Well it seems to me, Headlice, that it would be best for you to join our little crew. I don't like the idea of you sitting out here all alone."

She smiled at the idea, but Bradley wasn't keen. They finished their desserts and Headlice said goodbye to the man in the ice cream hut. Then Grandpa lifted the two children into the saucer—which, all the while, had been hanging above them like a huge umbrella.

Finally, he stood on a chair to grab at the hatch and heaved himself up through the round opening.

SHARKS FROM OUTER SPACE

As soon as he got back on board, Bradley ran to Waldo and knocked him away from the periscope. They'd left him behind when they went for ice cream. This was partly because Bradley was anxious not to lose him, but also because he thought that tying a string around his middle too often might make him sore. He still looked a bit squashed, so Bradley made a mental note to ask Grandpa if he had a nit-comb to groom him back into shape.

He lifted the eyepiece and squinted down his nose at it. On one side, it was covered in tooth marks, and tiny chunks had been bitten out of it.

Nit-comb.

That reminded him. He turned to Headlice,

who was admiring Waldo as he sailed overhead.

"What's that?" she wondered.

"A star-pup," Bradley told her. "They live in outer space. He's called Waldo. He's mine," he finished proudly.

"He's so cute!" cried Headlice, running after him. "But he looks so stressed! What's wrong with him?"

"Oh, nothing," replied Bradley. He felt less awkward around Headlice now that he had something to talk about. "He's just a bit preoccupied. He's got stuff on his mind. You know. *Star-pup* stuff."

Headlice had Waldo cornered.

"What like?" she wondered—jumping up and trying to catch him.

Bradley shrugged.

"Dunno. I don't think anyone does. But I can tell you what'll happen when he works it out," he boasted.

Waldo flew away from them and hid above the sofa with his face to the wall.

"What?" wondered Headlice.

"He'll be this big," Bradley told her, holding his hands about a foot apart—"and all of a sudden, he'll stop, and sing a little song, and look very happy."

Headlice smiled.

"And then he'll explode."

"He'll *what?*" cried Headlice.

"He'll explode," repeated Bradley. "But don't worry—I think they enjoy it."

"Oh, *yuck*," said Headlice with relish. "Think of the mess! Blood and fur—everywhere!"

"Oh, no—nothing like that," he assured her. "Just baby star-pups."

"Really? Oh Bradley!"

She lunged for him without warning and threw her arms wide open.

"That's adorable! I could *kiss* you!" she cried.

Bradley jumped with fright. Luckily, before she could catch him, the saucer lurched up into the air and they were suddenly weightless.

Headlice seemed delighted to be floating around. She was obviously an old pro, and could propel herself up and down the cabin with consummate ease. Bradley watched her somersaulting overhead, surprised by how easy she seemed to find it.

After a while, she glanced sideways at him.

"I *could* kiss you," she reminded him darkly.

Eventually, Grandpa had some words with Captain Nosegay and left the console. All three of them sat on the sofa to play cards.

"You know you and me are about the same age," said Headlice quite suddenly. "And I *did* save your life. Maybe you could repay me by taking me out some time?"

Slowly, it dawned on Bradley that she was talking to him.

"What—like a date?" He looked around and floundered. "But—but don't you think we're a bit young for that sort of thing?"

"Well maybe," she agreed. "But space is pretty empty. I've only met one other boy and he had tentacles. Who knows when the next eligible bachelor will come along?"

"I see," said Bradley—blushing bright red. "But look. The thing is, I'm generally used to girls having more *eyes*."

And then he folded his arms unhappily as if to say, *Well there. I said it.*

She frowned and touched her face.

"Oh. So *that's* why you kept staring at me," she muttered. "I thought you were checking me out."

Bradley stared unhappily at the floor. Suddenly, Grandpa nudged him in the ribs.

"What's wrong with you lad? I'll give you some money! You can take her bowling!" he suggested.

Bradley covered his face.

"Please, Grandpa—shut up!" he cried in despair.

When he finally looked up, he saw that Headlice was staring right at him.

"So you think I need more eyes," she said flatly.

He pulled his hair.

"Look—I'm not saying you need to go crazy," he assured her. "One more would do the trick."

She grinned—and then, fanning the cards to

make one vanish unexpectedly, said, "But I *do* have another eye. Just not on my face."

"Not on your—?"

He covered his mouth in horror. He just hoped that it wouldn't come worming out of her ear, or appear suddenly on the tip of her tongue.

"In fact," she told him—reaching out to produce the card from behind his ear—"I must have about fifty. They cover my back—like huge pimples!"

He turned green, but she just laughed and shuffled the cards.

"Only joking!" she assured him.

Bradley didn't laugh. He wondered where exactly the joke had started, and whether she really *did* have another eye somewhere. When she got up from the sofa and floated weightlessly away, he had the horrible idea that a bright, blinking eye might appear suddenly on the back of her head.

There was a long silence. After a while, Grandpa clapped his hands on his knees.

"Well! *This* is awkward," he observed brightly—and he went off to fetch them supper.

The next morning—if the idea of morning meant anything by now—the fluorescent strips flickered into life. Bradley yawned and rubbed his eyes. When he opened them, he saw that Grandpa was frowning at the console.

"What a joke," the old man muttered, half to himself. "What an absolute faff. Here, Bradley—are you awake?—you are *not* going to believe this."

Bradley yawned and scratched his neck.

"Why? What's happened?"

Grandpa shook his head and grinned stupidly.

"It's this bloomin' spaceship. It's been in first gear all along! Look—there's another gear. A whole second gear that we haven't been using!"

He pressed a button, and something went *PING!*

"Blistering black holes—there's a third one too! I *thought* it was a bit slow for a brand new saucer. I suppose I should've read the manual!"

Bradley floated over.

"So what does third gear mean? Is it three times as fast?"

Grandpa pulled at his moustache.

"Well I don't know how gears work on Earth," he said—"but actually, in this case, it's even faster than that. It's exponential. Look at this."

He pointed to some numbers on a round screen. Bradley followed his finger from left to right, but couldn't make sense of the strange flashing figures.

"Do you—do you think we ought to try it?" he wondered.

"Try it? What—now?"

Grandpa peered at a row of switches.

"Yes," he decided at last. "Yes. I think that would be an *excellent* idea. We should get to Grabelon much faster in third gear. In fifteen minutes' time, in fact."

Bradley spluttered with shock.

"Fifteen minutes? Why—we could've done the whole trip in half an hour!"

Grandpa just shrugged.

"You ought to wake Headlice," he said. "I'd hate for her to miss Saturn. It's *very* pretty."

Bradley woke Headlice, and they went to the largest of the round portholes together.

"Initialising second gear!" barked Grandpa from the console.

"Check!" added Bradley, for no real reason.

There was a slight lurch.

"Did it work?" asked Grandpa.

Bradley peered out at the stars, which seemed as motionless as ever.

"No idea. Try third," he suggested.

"Yessir!" said Grandpa sarcastically. "It's my spaceship, but you can give the orders! Aye aye, cap'n! Initialising third gear!"

There was a second, more violent lurch, which made Bradley bang his knee.

"Ouch," he muttered, rubbing it through his pyjama bottoms.

"Well?" said Grandpa.

Bradley looked through the porthole again. There was nothing to judge speed against, and, shrugging, he said as much.

Grandpa looked disappointed.

"Really? Well according to my calculations, we should be going fast. *Mind-numbingly* fast."

"Well *my* mind is *definitely* numb," said Headlice, rubbing her temples in the background. "What about you guys?"

Bradley ignored her.

"Well there should be a speedometer," he pointed out. "Shouldn't there?"

Grandpa shrugged.

"You'd think so, wouldn't you? On the other hand, there *should* be a special hull to protect us from deadly cosmic rays, and we're making do with the lagging I stole from your father's loft. Do tell him I'm sorry if the pipes burst. Let's see what the console says. Oh look, it's flashing."

He ran his finger across the screen.

"It says, *impact in five seconds,*" he announced.

Bradley looked up in alarm.

"Impact? What impact?" he wondered.

Before Grandpa could answer, a deafening

Bang! filled the cabin. Something had hit the outside of the saucer, denting the wall and shaking the green sofa half off its brackets. The cushions had achieved escape velocity during the impact and now floated three feet above it, with Waldo tumbling weightlessly among them.

Bradley grabbed onto the rail with both hands.

"What on earth was that?" he squeaked.

Grandpa pulled out a spotted hanky and shook it open.

"No idea!" he said faintly. "Nothing too important, I hope. Let me see the damage report."

He leaned forward to peer at the monitor again. Then made a small sound of dismay.

"That was a NASA probe. It's called the Cassini orbiter," he explained.

Behind his head, the remains of the probe began to stream past the round windows. Broken bits of casing and circuitry sparkled in the starlight, all looking very expensive.

"Remember you were meant to say sorry to your father if the pipes burst?" added Grandpa.

Bradley nodded.

"Well you might want to say sorry to NASA while you're at it."

Bradley covered his eyes and groaned.

"But not to worry," said Grandpa brightly. "Hello—what's this?" He leaned forward to read the monitor again. "*Impact in five seconds?*" he murmured.

"What—*again?*" said Bradley in disbelief.

Moments later came a loud *Pop!*—followed by another, and another, and another. Before long, an endless low rumble filled the cabin. It sounded like a monsoon, or popcorn popping.

Very slowly, Grandpa and Bradley turned to the front of the cabin. With each little *Pop!* a tiny round dent appeared in the hull. Soon, the whole wall was dotted with them.

"Sweet rings of Saturn!" cried Grandpa. "We must be flying through—well—the actual rings of Saturn!"

He yanked a lever. They dipped towards the floor as the saucer shot upwards. At last, they cleared the rings and the noise subsided.

Bradley glimpsed Saturn briefly at a porthole, but already it was racing away from them—strange and yellow against the black backdrop of space.

Grandpa shook his head.

"Too close for comfort!" he croaked. "I suppose I'd better read the damage report, eh?"

He pressed his face close to the monitor.

"Good grief," he muttered, blinking short-sightedly. "*Impact in five seconds? Again?*"

Bradley was astonished.

"What—*another* one?" he managed weakly.

Grandpa laughed.

"Ha ha! Only joking! What a card! Oh wait, it *does* say—"

PRANK! went the spaceship—flipping violently as it glanced off something big. For a split second, the portholes were filled with a busy grey blur. Then it was gone.

"By the Great Red Spot!" swore Grandpa. "We just grazed the side of Methone—one of Saturn's moons! Just *imagine* if we'd hit it head-on!"

He shook his head.

"I'm sorry," he announced firmly, "but that's the final straw. I'm putting it back in first gear."

Bradley opened his mouth to object, but before he could, he felt someone prodding his shoulder. He turned to see a single blue eye admiring him from point blank range.

It was Headlice.

"Hey—did you *see* Saturn?" she said giddily. "I can't believe how big it was! It must have been twice the size of my asteroid!"

He looked at her oddly.

"Are you kidding? It's *much* bigger than an asteroid. It's a planet. Planets are huge. Don't you remember how big Pluto was?"

She shrugged.

"Not really," she said. "I mean it *seemed* big enough, but everything looks bigger when you're small—doesn't it?"

For the rest of the day, Grandpa refused to move out of first gear. When Bradley and Headlice begged him to, he got annoyed and went to have a sulk in the storage cupboard.

"If you want to go speeding," he called out to the pair of them, "you can darn well drive it yourself. No, no—it's fine. Honestly, it's fine. You're in charge now. I hope you're happy. I'm sure you'll be very good at it. Enjoy."

Hours later, Pluto appeared at a porthole. It was moving so slowly that it was hard to tell it moved at all, and Bradley was surprised by how cold and dead it looked. It was like a bit of old wax, stuck to the sky and starting to crumble. One large moon and two tiny ones littered the sky like crumbs beside it. It was hardly the most exciting thing in the world, but it *was* the perfect excuse to educate Headlice, so he took her to a window and pointed it out.

"It just looks small because it's far away," he explained. "It's actually enormous. In fact, if you landed on it, there would be nothing but Pluto as far as you could see."

"Wow. Pluto's really that big?"

"Well you should know," he said gently. "You *were* born there."

Then he turned and looked at her.

"You know where I come from, *Headlice* isn't really a suitable name for a girl," he pointed out. "What does it mean in Plutonian?"

"What, literally?"

She gestured towards her blonde curls.

"It's a kind of bug that lays eggs in your hair," she explained.

After an hour or two, which Bradley filled by running after Waldo, Grandpa emerged from the cupboard. He seemed to have cheered up immensely.

"Grabelon's next door to Pluto," he told them brightly—"so we should be seeing it any minute now!"

He was about to add something, but before he could, Captain Nosegay came noisily to life. The dome opened, exposing the floating brain, and something like the horn of a gramophone swivelled to face them.

"Warning!" barked the Captain.

"What's wrong with him?" wondered Bradley.

"Prob'ly just a false alarm," said Grandpa. "I

think we've hit all the things we're going to hit today. Space is pretty empty here."

But the Captain's huge nose was trembling.

"*Nostrils detect disturbance in the Solar Winds!*" he insisted in a robotic voice.

Grandpa rolled his eyes.

"Now now!" he reminded the Captain good-naturedly—"whoever smelt it, dealt it! And as for you children—you'd better keep an eye out for Grabelon."

Bradley and Headlice were at opposite ends of the cabin. They kicked themselves over and ended up at the same porthole. Grandpa went to the controls and explained that he would turn the ship around to get a good view of Grabelon.

There was a long, long silence.

"*Whoever said the rhyme did the crime,*" muttered the Captain sourly.

They ignored him. Eventually, Grandpa turned from the console and said, "Voilà!"

Bradley scratched his neck. He wasn't sure what to say.

"It's *beautiful*," cooed Headlice eventually.

Bradley crossed his arms.

"There's nothing there," he said flatly.

Headlice glared at him.

"Don't be so rude!" she hissed. "Say something nice!"

But Bradley was unmoved.

"There's *nothing* there," he insisted.

"Nothing where?" wondered Grandpa.

He had floated up behind them. Outside the porthole was nothing but stars.

"Oh. I guess I got it wrong. Another moment, I'm sure."

Suddenly, something strange happened. The darkness shimmered like hot air, and a globe of light appeared out of nowhere.

Bradley rubbed his eyes. It was as if the whole planet had been hidden with a dark cloth, waiting for someone to unveil it with a proud flourish. It troubled him, slightly, to think of a whole planet hidden in space—covered in darkness like a birdcage with a blanket—but Grabelon was also very beautiful; and when he shivered, he couldn't tell one feeling from the other.

Grandpa looked relieved.

"Grabelon," he announced.

Bradley pressed his face to the glass. It didn't look much like the other planets. It was dark—as dark as the starry field behind it—but sequinned all over with brilliant lights.

"Now *that's* beautiful," said Bradley. "How long before we land, Grandpa?"

Grandpa didn't answer. He had the side of his face squashed against a porthole.

"Grandpa?" ventured Bradley again.

The old man didn't respond. He stared back the way they'd come from, muttering softly to himself.

"Impossible!" he hissed. "Not *them* again! This close to home? Never!"

"What?" pressed Bradley. "What can you see?"

"I'm not quite sure," muttered Grandpa. "Sometimes I wish space had *air,* so I could just wind the window down and stick my head out! But I think I saw—there! Yes, there!"

He rounded on Bradley, and the look on his face was so fearful that Bradley actually shrank away from him. His eyes were very wide, and his mouth, which seemed to have shrunk, was cowering with fright beneath his white whiskers.

"We have to get away," he whispered. "*Now.*"

Without another word, he kicked himself to the main console—so hard that, if he hadn't caught it, he would have carried on and smacked the far wall.

"But what *is* it?" insisted Bradley, pressing his own face to the porthole.

Suddenly, in the corner of his eye, he thought he saw something—something big and fierce like a killer whale. He tried to look directly at it, but every time he did, his eyes went funny.

"Cloaking device," said Grandpa tersely. "That's why we didn't spot 'em. Why," he suddenly realised—"I should have listened to the Captain, shouldn't I? We couldn't *see* them, but he *smelt* 'em—caught a whiff of 'em, cutting through the Solar Winds! Anyway, they try to hide until they're very close—and then—"

Whatever it was, he couldn't bear to say it. Instead, he dragged a finger from ear to ear, and made a gory noise at the back of his throat.

A split second later, the other ship snapped horribly into focus.

Bradley couldn't help staring. Apart from a line of flashing red lights, which frowned beneath a sort of a snout, the surface of the ship was completely bare. It had no windows. It looked very sinister, like a fish from the bottom of a sunless sea.

Bradley rounded on Grandpa.

"What *is* it?" he demanded.

Grandpa shook his head.

"You don't want to know," he whispered.

Bradley's blood ran suddenly cold.

"*No one* knows," added Grandpa, flipping switches up and down. "Not really. They come from *outside the Solar System*—across miles and miles of empty space! We call them pirates, but they're nothing like Earth pirates." He wiped his face and flicked away a handful of sweat. "They're worse," he warned—"*much* worse."

Bradley stared at the other ship. A hatch had opened, and strange black shapes were tumbling out. One by one, they uncurled into horrible dark figures. Bradley couldn't tear his eyes away. They looked vaguely human, insofar as they had arms and legs, but their heads were pointed instead of round. He couldn't see their faces, which seemed like a mercy—but then, with a shiver, he wondered if they even *had* faces.

One by one, the strange things fell from sight.

"Quick!" squeaked Bradley, flapping his hands. "Third gear! Now!"

But Grandpa's head was shaking. In fact, his whole body was shaking, but his head was shaking in a different way—the very specific way that means *No.*

"Grandpa!" snapped Bradley. His heart was pounding, but he tried to stay calm. "Now look. I know you didn't like it when we went fast—but a load of men came out of that ship, and I think they want to get us!"

Towards the end of the sentence, his voice had

gone very squeaky. Grandpa made eye contact with him, and his face was dire—but he managed to squeeze out an embarrassed smile.

"Well!" he managed. "Heh heh! You're not going to *believe* what silly old Grandpa's done now!"

The smile faded from his face.

"I've forgotten how I found them," he admitted quietly. "The other gears, I mean."

Bradley opened his mouth but never got chance to reply. Suddenly, a horrible *banging* came from the floor—a dreadful insistent *thumping,* as if countless fists were pounding on the bottom of the ship.

Bradley saw something at a porthole and glanced over. Suddenly, Headlice began to scream—because there, peering into the cabin...

Everything seemed to slow down, as if time had turned to treacle. When Bradley saw the face at the window, he felt a rumble at the bottom of his chest. His heart beat once—and then a second time—as SOMETHING *scrabbled up his windpipe. When it emerged from his mouth, he found that it wasn't a*

THING *at all, but rather a* SOUND, *and the sound went—*

"AARGH!" screamed Bradley.

He shrank from the porthole in fright. The thing looking in at them was horrible—the stuff of nightmares. It must have crawled up from the great dark dungeons of the universe. It had a huge conical head, with razor-sharp teeth and two round eyes.

And what terrible eyes they were. They reflected the darkness of space but none of the sparkle.

It looked like a shark. Instead of fins, it had powerful grey arms, which pounded the glass with strong grey fists. From the neck down, it wore a suit made of greasy metal.

The eyes made Bradley's blood run cold. There was something about them that seemed alert and alive, but mindless and manic—like ants crawling on a blade of grass.

Suddenly, everything went windy.

"Get out!" roared Grandpa.

Bradley span on the spot, and saw, to his

horror, that two grey hands had forced the hatch open. A pointy head popped into view, gnashing huge white teeth in all directions.

"I said get *out!*" cried Grandpa again. He grabbed the periscope, twirled around it like a dancer, and shot himself off into the cupboard. Then he came straight back out, wielding the extending ladder like a huge club.

The rush of air sucked him to the hatch. With an ear-splitting roar, he swung the ladder overhead and hammered the very top of the intruder's skull.

"Take that!" he cried.

The pirate looked surprised as it tumbled out into space. Grandpa grinned at Bradley, straddling the hatch with his legs so he wouldn't be blown out. Moments later, a much larger head roared up into the cabin, snapping at his crotch.

"What?—why!—sweet rings of Saturn!" bellowed Grandpa.

He sprang high into the air and swung the ladder a second time.

"Take that!" he roared again.

Bradley, who had struggled with the same ladder back on Earth, wondered how Grandpa could swing it so effortlessly—but they were in space now, of course, and it suddenly dawned on him that the ladder would be weightless.

Meanwhile, in Grandpa's hands, it had become a formidable weapon. It raced towards the pirate's skull, but a grey hand shot up to block it. In the monster's powerful grip, the metal rung buckled like a fizzy drinks can.

Headlice sprang into action, determined to help. She bounced around the cabin, stopping only to throw a cushion or something equally useless at the pirate. Before long, it was half-buried in junk, with its legs still dangling out of the hatch. It roared in annoyance, trying to shake Grandpa off the end of the ladder so it could climb fully inside.

Keeping one hand on the wall, Bradley reached out to grab Headlice by the wrist.

"Calm down!" he told her firmly.

His mind was beginning to race. He watched

the weightless ladder rip and tear in the pirate's hands. As he did, he pictured himself back on Earth, finishing a can of pop. Crushing it between his fingers.

Weightless, he thought uselessly. Pop.

Then his eyes widened. *He had an idea.*

His eyes darted to the sofa, where they'd left the bottle of Gee Whiz Soda. The artificial gravity drink! It stared back at him, propped up between two cushions—full of shimmering bubbles and rushing colours.

"Grab something!" he told Headlice.

She held onto the rail with both hands. He made his way along the wall, resisting the wind that sucked at his legs. It wasn't as strong as it had been, because the pirate was partly blocking the hatch—but air was still escaping at an alarming rate.

When he got to the sofa, he grabbed the bottle. Then he let go of the sofa, hugging the bottle to his chest. He was dragged away in a heartbeat, caught by a whirlpool of escaping air. He circled the hatch, getting closer and closer to the pirate's jaws.

Everything slowed down again. He was surprised by how calm he felt.

He looked at the pirate and noticed, for the first time, the jagged white scar that streaked down its face. Then he saw something that sparkled under its chin...

("Bradley!" roared Grandpa. "What are you doing?!")

Bradley's eyes widened. It was covered in engine oil, and barely recognisable under all the grime, but it was definitely a *silver locket.*

He remembered the story that Grandpa had told him back in the Asteroid Belt. The story of a scarred pirate, who'd ripped a silver locket from around his neck...

It was the same one, Bradley realised. It *had* to be.

"Get off our spaceship!" he shouted bravely.

The pirate released the ladder and swivelled to face him, gnashing rows of razor-sharp teeth.

"Bradley!" cried Grandpa again.

Bradley ignored him. He fumbled with the

bottle of Gee Whiz, unscrewing the cap. Then he *aimed the bottle and squeezed it hard.*

It glugged. A round fizzy mass erupted from the bottle and sailed towards the pirate's face.

The pirate looked surprised and shut its mouth—but not fast enough. Some of the drink went through its teeth and down its throat. The rest smashed into shimmering orbs that foamed and fizzed and were blown into space.

The horrible eyes bulged brightly with fear. It knew straight away that something was wrong. Almost instantly, it had become *very heavy.* It dropped awkwardly and struggled to stop itself falling through the hatch.

"Genius!" cried Grandpa with approval. His voice sounded muffled, as if there wasn't much air left.

Bradley threw the bottle to one side, then planted his feet on the floor and kicked with all his might. As he somersaulted over the pirate's head, he reached down—grabbed the locket by the chain—and yanked it clean off.

Where the chain snapped, tiny silver links

came loose and shot into space.

The pirate roared a terrible roar...

...and the last of the air began to swirl away.

Suddenly, Headlice lost her grip on the rail. Her one eye widened as she fell towards the hatch, desperately clutching at thin air.

"Headlice!" cried Bradley. His lungs emptied as he mouthed her name.

With his last drop of energy, he managed to catch her by the ankle. As he did, the pirate glared up at them—tried to grab Bradley's foot—but *lost its grip and fell instantly from sight.*

Bradley and Headlice nearly went flying out after it. For a second, there was nothing between them and outer space. Somehow, he managed to straddle the open hatch with his feet and keep both of them inside the cabin.

He pulled Headlice close and held her awkwardly. Then he looked down. The pirate was plummeting away into nowhere.

Below them, infinity stretched downwards forever—sparkling like black marble.

Then the hatch snapped shut, and all was still.

* * *

Immediately, there was a fierce rushing sound. Fresh air was filling the cabin from countless tiny nozzles. The remaining pirates continued to hammer on the hatch but soon gave up. Just as Bradley was about to pass out, he realised he could breathe again.

They drifted around in a deep stunned silence, recovering from the ordeal. Eventually, Headlice burst into giddy applause. Waldo (who had somehow escaped being blown into space) came out of the cupboard looking very worried.

"Brilliant!" declared Grandpa. He floated over and gave Bradley a high five, which propelled them both to opposite ends of the cabin. "That's teamwork!" he added—giving him a thumbs-up.

But Bradley wasn't listening. He was looking through the porthole, to where the pirates had appeared in their horrible ship. The ship was still there, but rays of red light were striking it and shooting past it. Bradley thought that they

145

might be lasers, but it was hard to tell without any sort of noise. Would lasers even *make* a noise, he wondered dimly? Meanwhile, the remaining pirates hung back from their ship, as if they were too scared to go near it.

Bradley watched through the window. Suddenly, the pirate's ship vanished in a soundless explosion, and two figures came swooping out of nowhere. Between them, they held a silvery net, which stretched like a lady's stocking. They moved very fast, wrapping up the pirates, then dragged them out of sight.

"That must be the space police," explained Grandpa. He coughed and wiped something from his lips. "Better late than never, eh?"

Bradley pressed his face to the porthole. There were no more lasers. All he could see was a dark spaceship with flashing blue lights.

"I wonder if they'll want a statement?" wondered Grandpa.

Bradley shrugged. He wasn't too bothered either way. Just grateful, and glad that they were safe.

FAR FROM HOME

SUDDENLY, BRADLEY NOTICED that Grandpa was in a great deal of pain, and doing his best to hide it from him.

"What's wrong?" he asked.

The old astronaut looked down at himself. There was a rip in his breastplate with blood on the sharp edges. He gripped them in his gloved hands, grunted, and pulled them apart.

"Oh dear," he muttered.

Bradley couldn't believe his eyes. The pirate must have bitten through the metal. Behind Grandpa's breastplate, everything was greasy with bright red blood.

"You're hurt!" gasped Bradley—amazed that he hadn't noticed. "When did it happen?"

Grandpa shrugged and tried to smile.

"Not sure. It was all so fast. When you went to the sofa, I think."

His smile became a grimace.

"I thought I was a goner," he admitted. "But then you did your trick with the fizzy pop, and all was saved!"

Bradley was appalled. As Grandpa talked, more and more blood bubbled out of his chest. It looked very deep and very painful.

"We need to get you to a hospital," said Bradley quickly. "A—a *space* hospital. Is there such a thing as a space hospital?"

He grabbed fistfuls of his hair and turned to Headlice. There were spaceships and space suits and space pirates, he reasoned desperately, and even space police. It would be strange— illogical!—if there wasn't a single space hospital.

"*Surely* there's such a thing as a space hospital," he pointed out.

"Never mind space hospital," said Headlice firmly. "There isn't time. Bring him here and I'll do the Heimlich manoeuvre."

She began to roll up her sleeves, but Grandpa

shook his head.

"No need, no need," he assured her, waving a hand.

He floated to the storage cupboard and shut the door behind him. Bradley covered his mouth and looked at Headlice.

"It's really bad," he told her. He could feel that he had gone quite pale.

She just beamed.

"Don't worry," she told him. "We'll patch him up somehow!"

Before he could reply, the cupboard door *whooshed* open and Grandpa drifted out again. He looked very pale, but smiled bravely and waved a tub of pills.

"Here they are!" he told them—fumbling with the lid. "*Mooncat's Multi-Purpose.* Let's give 'em a whirl."

Bradley gave the wall a gentle push. He floated over and peered at the label, which read, *Mooncat's Multi-Purpose Miracle Pills. Contains: Guarana, Extract of Charonian Cat-Blossom, Cod Liver Oil, Penicillin, Titanian Wobble-Wood, and*

Mooncat's SECRET INGREDIENT. *Cures 78% of everything.* DISCLAIMER: *Will not cure death.*

Bradley wasn't impressed. He looked up at Grandpa, who was shaking two pink pills into a trembling hand.

"Now look," he told him firmly. "You've got a *serious injury.* We don't have time for these stupid pills. We need to apply pressure to the wound and get you to—to a *space* hospital!"

But Grandpa shook his head.

"They've worked before," he assured him—"and fingers crossed, they'll work again!"

He opened his mouth and dropped the pills onto his tongue. As he did, Bradley saw that there was blood on his teeth.

"Honestly Grandpa," he said quietly. "It looks really bad."

Grandpa just rolled his eyes, wiped his lips, and gulped the pills down in one go.

He blinked and smiled.

"I feel better already!" he declared.

He patted his breastplate, leaving a greasy red hand-print.

"Mark my words," he insisted—as blood continued to squelch and bubble from the awful injury. "They're definitely working!"

Bradley covered his mouth.

"Grandpa," he began—"I honestly think we should find the nearest—"

But he didn't finish. Already, he could see that something magical was happening. Suddenly, the blood seemed to be trickling *back into Grandpa's body,* and the injury was undergoing an impossible transformation. In fact, it was shrinking before their very eyes.

"See?" said Grandpa.

As the injury repaired itself, it made a strange sort of *sizzling* sound—like frying bacon. Bradley couldn't tear his eyes away. It was magical and disgusting at the same time.

"Mooncat's Multi-Purpose," said Grandpa in admiration. "What a product!"

Before long, apart from a bit of dried blood and a small pink scar, the wound had vanished completely. Bradley was amazed, but Grandpa seemed quite blasé about it. In fact, now that his chest had healed, he seemed more worried about his damaged breastplate.

"What a shame," he muttered—fingering the ripped edges. "But never mind. I'll pop into Wuztop Nash on the way back to Earth. They do alterations and repairs While-U-Wait."

Bradley looked at him, and then at Headlice.

"Never mind the space suit!" he pointed out. "I can't believe what I just saw! It was amazing! *And* weird."

Grandpa smiled.

"Get used to it!" he told him. "You'll see plenty of things more amazing than that, young Bradley. Weirder ones, too!"

A little while later, something occurred to Bradley.

"Look at this," he told Grandpa—showing him the dirty locket. "Is this the one you lost?"

Grandpa's face lit up.

"By Jupiter!" he cried. "It is! It really is!"

The three of them gathered round while he prised it open. Inside was a tiny photo of a beautiful woman, with a wicked smile and a gleam in her eyes.

"I miss her dreadfully," admitted Grandpa. "It's my own fault for leaving, of course—but I hate to be stuck in one place. What is it you say on Earth? The grass is always greener? Well on Grabelon, we say *the stars are always brighter.* That sums me up, really. Always waiting for the next adventure! Still—if I didn't get itchy feet, I wouldn't have come to Earth in the first place. She was a fine woman, though. A darned fine woman."

When Bradley realised who it was, he could hardly believe his eyes.

"Blimey," he said—taking a closer look. "That's Grandma, isn't it? She's beautiful!"

"Mm. She was."

Grandpa smiled down at the tiny picture for some time. Then he closed the locket very carefully and stashed it away inside his suit.

"And she still is—for an older gal!" he finished with a wink.

* * *

Before long, it was time to land on Grabelon—which, all the while, had watched them through a porthole, shimmering coldly like a mirror-ball.

Bradley went to see. The surface of the planet became a dark horizon curving beneath them. Everything in the cabin sank gently downwards and settled like silt on the floor. Through the porthole, he could make out a lumpy skyline— but everything was hazy, as if partially obscured by a net curtain. Then they descended from the clouds, and the whole city shot into focus.

Bradley stared this way and that, pressing his face to the porthole. The architecture on Grabelon was very *strange*. It was decidedly *blobby*, as if someone's idea of building a city was to make play-dough balls and stick them on top of one another. In fact, rather than being built, the city seemed to have grown like a coral reef. Here and there, between the crazy leaning towers, were strange shapes that breathed like bellows, spewing coloured fumes into the air.

Bradley felt Headlice press his hand.

"I see what you mean," she told him—"about them being *huge*, I mean."

Bradley stared at her. He tried to untangle his hand and left her holding a single finger.

"About *what* being huge?" he wondered.

She smiled prettily and squeezed it.

"Planets!" she reminded him.

"Oh." He grinned stupidly. "Right," he muttered.

He returned his attention to the view outside. It was spectacular. The dark buildings rose from a soupy green fog that looked like a swamp. Their little round windows were very bright, and fairy lights had been strung between them like washing lines. It looked like Blackpool Illuminations, only transported back to the dawn of time. The buildings were like dinosaurs wading through it. They bowed their heads, puzzled by the extravaganza of light that surrounded them.

"This is Old Saturn Town," explained Grandpa. "If you like music, you'll *love* Old Saturn Town!"

"I wonder what it's like in the daytime?" wondered Bradley.

Grandpa laughed over the controls.

"Look at the sky," he told him.

Bradley peered upwards, pressing his nose to the round window. Through the clouds, it was hard to see anything, but he could just make out a couple of stars.

"One of those is the sun," said Grandpa unexpectedly. "I couldn't even tell you which, off the top of my head. We're very far from home, Bradley. There *is* no day on Grabelon."

Bradley shivered and said, "Oh."

"Oh indeed!" replied Grandpa. "Now get ready. It's time to land."

He returned his attention to one of the monitors. Bradley stayed by the porthole, trying to work out which one of the tiny stars was the sun. Each seemed as cold and remote as the next.

"You know, I reckon we've crammed a lot in to our holiday so far," added Grandpa from the console. "What with Mars and the Asteroid Belt and the pirates. It's been quite an adventure, hasn't it?"

Bradley nodded.

"Definitely," he agreed with feeling. "It's been great."

"Good," said Grandpa. "But listen. I want you to know that we've only just begun. Why—we've barely even scratched the surface! You see, Grabelon isn't just *any* planet. It's *my* planet. It's a secret planet—a planet of peril and adventure—and I *can't wait* to share it with you."

He flipped a switch and the lights went off in the cabin, making the ones outside seem even brighter. Bradley turned his attention back to the window, not wanting to miss a moment of the view.

"It's going to be great," he agreed.

Here and there, fireworks lit up small pockets of the strange skyline. An enormous glitter cannon discharged itself suddenly in the distance. The crisp *POP!* reached them moments later as the glitter came down like snow. Then it was gone. Bradley wondered whether they were celebrating something in particular, or just had fireworks and glitter cannons every night.

He turned from the window and saw that Grandpa was grinning at him.

"Welcome to Grabelon," said the intrepid old astronaut. "Now hold on tight! I'm taking her down."

And with a twinkle in his eye, he grabbed a long lever and pulled it hard.

TO BE CONTINUED...

Stay tuned for another thrilling instalment of this epic adventure! Hold on for dear life as our intrepid heroes brave squishy space food, arachnid assassins, and a dinghy race over deadly water!

Where are you going?! Come back, for pity's sake, and find out what happens in...

The forthcoming sensational sequel to...

THE ASTRONAUT'S APPRENTICE!

5983903R00095

Printed in Great Britain
by Amazon.co.uk, Ltd.,
Marston Gate.